ON THE ROOF

WITH WORDS WE WEAVE

2024 ANTHOLOGY

TEXAS HIGH PLAINS WRITERS

CONTENTS

INTRODUCTION

"Nothing is impossible. The word itself says, 'I'm possible!'"
— *Audrey Hepburn*

If there's one thing writers and people living in the Texas panhandle know all too well, it's that nothing is impossible. However, for a writer, there is sometimes doubt. We are alone, sitting with our thoughts, uncertainties, and story ideas, in search of that perfect word as we stare at the waiting page. Yet, despite the solitary pursuit, the goal is to share our stories with others.

Enter the Texas High Plains Writers anthology: With Words We Weave.

Now in its fifth year, the anthology provides both challenges and opportunities to members and entertainment for readers. Challenge via a new theme each year and opportunity to share our stories with the world and see them in print. For some, it's their first published work.

This year, many of us have been looking forward to seeing what tales our members came up with for the "On the Roof" theme. Knowing the talent in our organization, I have no doubt the variety will be cleverly creative.

Enjoy!
Donna Rosson
Texas High Plains Writers President 2023

ONE
SMOKE AND MIRRORS

KATE BAILEY

Dinal looked around at the sleepy oasis town slowly coming to life. A bell cut through the songs of the morning birds. It didn't sing to welcome the sun, but to raise the people from their beds and call them to pray.

Not particularly religious, Dinal continued on his way to the market. The tall buildings on either side of the street boasted six or seven floors, each with windows looking out over the hills of the city. He walked over to the bright-blue banners signifying the entrance of the bazaar. It would have been marvelous any other day, but today he had to walk around the wooden beams of scaffolding.

Beautiful banners in bright purples and reds and oranges and greens hung over the rafters, blocking the withering glare of the sun from the shoppers and the merchants. A few of the early vendors already had their shops set up and were rising from the ground and rolling up their prayer rugs.

Letting his eyes shift from booth to booth, Dinal spotted his partner leaning against the clay wall of a building, eating an apple, one he definitely didn't pay for. Buni raised his chin in acknowledgment but otherwise didn't move from his shaded corner.

The third member of their crew would be here closer to time.

Dinal wandered through the bazaar as the crowds became thicker and the sun became hotter. Sweat dripped from beneath the turban on his head, but Dinal simply wiped his forehead and kept going. He shared small talk with the visitors and the locals alike, as if he were just meandering his day away. But he and Buni were here for a very specific purpose.

One by one, guards began to loiter in the area, their white and gold clothing making them clearly stand out. They were unlike the browns that he wore, something specifically meant for him to blend in.

One, two, three, four of them stood with wary eyes on their surroundings. This was twice the number of guards he had been expecting, but instead of warning Dinal away from the area, it made him even more curious.

The artifact was here.

But the question was, which of these vendors was the one selling it?

Buni appeared at his side like a scorpion slipping out from under the shade of a rock. "That one." He jutted his chin toward the far corner under the violet banners. "Tell Celeste to look at his wares."

Then Buni was gone again, disappearing into the crowd that was now brushing shoulder against shoulder.

The murmur of the crowds changed, and a smile pulled at Dinal's lips before he even turned around. Celeste strode through the bazaar with the crowd parting on either side of her. The light blue of her dress and the shayla covering her hair made everyone stop and stare for a moment, as if she were the purest of the skies and her smile a beam of the sun cutting through the clouds.

But Dinal stared for another reason. As her gaze slid over to meet his, her eyebrows rose slightly and a smirk rested on her lips. He shifted his eyes to the merchant's booth Buni had indicated.

In this game of smoke and mirrors, she was the smoke and he and Buni were the mirrors.

Dinal circled around, sensing Buni near him but not in his line of sight.

The merchant held a silver lamp in his hand as he talked about the inscription on it and the myths surrounding it. Desert genies. Mischievous wish-granters. And vengeful captives.

Dinal didn't believe one thing the merchant said…all stories to make the price go up when the haggling started.

"It is said that Sultan Ali used this himself to gain his position of power." The merchant's tale was winding down. "But what would a beautiful woman like yourself wish for if she held it in her hands?"

The merchant's fingers were curled around the handle and the bottom. He held it just out of Celeste's reach, as if wanting her to lean forward farther into his story and the deal.

"I don't know." Celeste's voice whispered gently like the wind off the oasis. "I would need to hold it myself before I gained such inspiration."

Dinal took a step closer. As many times as they had pulled off a scheme like this, the flitter of adrenaline still ran through his body and made his breath catch. Or maybe it was the excitement of the money they were going to make off it.

The merchant clicked his tongue and shook his head. "I can't have you unleashing the magic until you buy it. This is how it goes."

Celeste took a step back and glanced at the crowd that had gathered around her. Upon her attention, they each scurried back to their business among the shops, leaving only her, Dinal, and Buni with their focus on the merchant and his prized lamp.

"And I can't buy it unless I know the magic's real."

The merchant hesitated a moment, his fingers red as they gripped a little tighter. But Dinal knew this was all a ploy.

Daring one last glance around, Dinal kept an eye on the guards. One had moved closer to a commotion at the far end, where the yellow banners led up to the sultan's palace. Two others were on the far side of the crowd. While their gazes still watched this area, it would take too long for them to do anything by the time Dinal grabbed the prize.

But the fourth guard was nowhere to be seen.

Maybe he had gone to the well to get a drink on this sweltering day. Or maybe he had moved on and was patrolling some other part of the city. But still, the fact that Dinal couldn't see him nagged at the back of his brain.

It didn't matter. Their plan was about to be put into action, and now was not the time for hesitation.

"Fine," the merchant relented. "Once you wrap your fingers around this prize, you will know its full worth."

"I have no doubt." Celeste reached out and grabbed the lamp.

The merchant's entire focus was on Celeste. Her smoke had obstructed his view of her two accomplices.

Buni swept in from the side, knocking into her, and the lamp

4

slipped from her grasp. Dinal caught it and ran in the opposite direction.

The merchant and Celeste yelled after him, but he ducked through the crowd, slipping off his turban and discarding the tunic he had wrapped around his shoulders. He grabbed a satchel from one of the nearby shops he had spied earlier and slipped the lamp inside.

Now that he had changed his appearance, he slowed to a walk. The guards would be looking for movement, and while he wanted to be out of there now, he knew the best way to escape was to use the crowd to his advantage.

That was, until the fourth guard stepped from the stall in front of him. His eyes flicked from Dinal to the satchel and back, catching him in the theft of the bag.

Dread coursed through his blood, and he turned on his heel and fled.

So much for his great escape plan.

Heading back toward the blue banners marking the entrance of the bazaar, Dinal raced through the crowd. His slender form slipped easily between the late-morning shoppers.

The shouting behind him was loud and drew the attention of even more guards. A sea of white and gold rushed toward him from both sides, and panic rose in Dinal's chest as he searched for a way out.

On his left, builders carried buckets of wet clay and straw to the roof, and the scaffolding they used to climb would work as the perfect escape.

Dinal grabbed onto the wooden structure and used his arms and legs to propel himself upward three, four, five, six floors above the murmuring crowd below him.

Curses flew at him from the workers as he bounded across the newly laid straw, landing on the rafters on the balls of his feet.

But his change of height didn't stop the chase. The ring of swords being unsheathed rang clearer than the earlier bells. But this time, they chimed his doom.

Setting his right hand on the railing bordering the roof, Dinal twisted into a flip that launched him five feet to the next building, where he landed with a second front flip, keeping his momentum going.

The rooftop in front of him was a maze of drying laundry. Something he could get lost in.

He swept aside a large white sheet with his left hand and cast a glance over his right shoulder to three guards jumping the gap to his current roof. But he had been sure more had been following him.

The whisper of a whistle zipped past his ear with an arrow slicing a hole in the white cloth inches from his hand.

The mix of heights across the rooftops made the chase fun, but it also gave advantage to the guards above him. And he couldn't forget about the archers.

Ducking to use the hanging clothes as cover, he continued across the roof, grateful that this one wasn't being worked on and his footing was sure.

Until it wasn't.

He pushed aside a pair of trousers and found himself staring at a ten-foot gap between the buildings.

It wasn't too terribly far, but the suddenness of the drop had stopped his momentum, his best tool.

Spinning around, he faced his opponents, now only a couple of strides away.

"Stop before you do something stupid!" one of the guards yelled.

Too late for that.

Dinal raised an eyebrow and took one step back, feeling the edge of the building against his foot.

The guard met the challenge by swinging his blade down through the rope that was holding the laundry.

Dinal grabbed the rope and leapt backward.

His stomach lurched with the feeling of weightless falling until the rope caught and his shoulders snapped with the sudden stop, followed by the smack of the clay building.

He groaned, trying to ignore the pain throbbing along his entire left side.

Digging his feet into the side of the building, he forced himself away and into an arching swing. There was no way he could get back up to the roof above him or the one on the other side of the alley, but the structural supports for the floor below stuck out like snakes peeking out of their holes.

Each one was barely wider than his foot, but between falling and being caught, he chose falling.

With a final swing, Dinal let go of the rope and flew through the air. He landed on the wooden structure with the ball of his left foot and kept running. Each step continuing his trajectory, but to where?

Dividing his attention between the steps quickly running out under him and his surroundings, he spotted an open window on the other wall, below him and to his right.

Crouching, he caught the next beam with his hands and swung sideways, aiming for the edge of the windowsill.

But he had miscalculated the distance.

His feet slipped past the opening, and his fingers bit into the windowsill, stopping his fall with a jar.

Arrows whizzed past him, one grazing his right arm, sending pain burning through him and threatening his grip on the windowsill.

With a kick of his feet, he was able to gain his traction again and swing in through the open window.

The smell of rising bread hung heavy in the air, reminding Dinal that he'd had to skip breakfast that morning. What they had been able to scrounge up for yesterday's dinner hadn't left enough for breakfast.

He ducked out of view of the window, and a baker cursed at the arrows which had followed him in. Dinal reached out, taking a loaf of bread in each hand, and stuffed them into his satchel.

Then he was out the opposite window, leaping through to roll onto the opposite rooftop. The walls of the city were coming up quickly, and he hadn't realized how much distance he had gone from the bazaar in the middle of town.

The problem was, there would be guards stationed on the walls to keep watch for invaders. He already had enough men chasing him today.

"Here!" Buni's voice carried to him from a nearby rooftop. "Throw me the satchel." Buni had also ditched his turban and looked enough like Dinal to draw the guards' attention.

Now was the time for the mirrors.

Dinal hurried to remove the satchel from around his shoulder. So far, he was still out of sight of the guards, but he had only seconds before they followed him through the bakery.

He pulled the lamp from his bag, casting one last glance at the loaves of bread, and tossed the satchel to Buni, who continued his run across the rooftops.

Dinal looked down at the windows below him, each eight feet below the other, all leading to the safety of the street.

With only his feet and one hand to catch him, he couldn't miss.

He leapt from the roof and landed before twisting and continuing his downward descent.

The cobblestone under his feet echoed his final landing, but shouts drew his attention back up as the forms of three guards vaulted across the gap to chase Buni.

Dinal let out a long breath, but he wasn't free and clear yet.

Jogging through the streets, he stopped on the far side of the yellow banners, just out of view from the sultan's palace. While he would have picked a more secluded rendezvous, Celeste was the one with the buyer and, therefore, the way to make money.

Her pale blue form stepped out of the shadows, her face turned away to stare at the palace.

Dinal finally let the tension drop from his shoulders as he held out the lamp to her. "I've got to say, that was the most thrilling chase in a long while."

"I'd say the same, too." The voice was deep, and as the figure in blue turned, Dinal's heart plummeted at the sight of a guard's thick beard. The adrenaline of the earlier chase was replaced with a deep-seated fear as he realized one thing.

He wasn't the only one playing with smoke and mirrors.

TWO
HOME SWEET HOME

KAREN BENCKENSTEIN

She lifted another large rock from its mossy bed to the top of the small wall. She took one step back to observe her progress. The spot she had chosen deep in the forest had been empty and flat. It now contained the beginnings of a small hut. This had better be worth it.

Just two weeks ago, Zelinda had been lounging in her luxury apartment on her designer bed. The sheets were silk so her hair wouldn't get tangled as she slept. The sound of hundreds of tinkling bells disturbed her sleep.

"Hello?" she mumbled into her cell phone.

"Zelinda? How can you be sleeping? Have you not seen social media? This contest is epic!"

Zelinda recognized the voice of her best friend Halee but was not following what she was talking about. "You know I have to get my twelve hours of beauty rest, Hals. What are you talking about?"

"There's a huge contest! The winner gets to stay at the Muladonald Mansion for a whole year. With a huge staff and an expense account!"

"What's the contest? What do I have to do to win?"

"Build a shelter and live in Blue Haven Forest for a week."

Zelinda looked down at her perfectly manicured nails. There was a small rhinestone in each ring fingernail. Her gaze shifted over to the eviction notice on her nightstand. It was stamped with a giant *30 DAYS*. She sighed. "I'm in."

The weeklong interview and audition process had been grueling. She had to get up each morning at *seven a.m.* and then often didn't get to sleep until after midnight. She had been interviewed on camera. She had taken a test on safety processes that had required a coaching session from her friend, Evan. She had built a popsicle shelter that stayed together for a whole two minutes.

When she finally got the call that she had been selected, she was too tired to jump for joy. She did bounce a little when she called Halee.

As she stepped back to look at her progress on the wall again, she was startled from her reverie by a low rumbling sound. At first, she thought it must be a huge truck. She could just see the large, burly man driving the truck. He would be here to save her. To build the shelter for her and help her stage the video to look like she had done all the work.

The video. She grimaced at the thought, then quickly rearranged her face into a peaceful smile. She knew 10,000 fans were watching her every move…or would be, once the producers had edited the footage. The other part of the contest was the YouTube video that would be created of her success or failure. This contest had the potential to not only set her up in a world-class mansion for a year but also make her a major influencer.

She lifted another rock. Three layers of rock were barely high enough to allow her to crawl in. But Zelinda decided it was enough. She peered at the sun through the trees; it would be dark soon. She hastily found a fallen tree branch with enough pine needles left on it to resemble coverage. She placed it across her small structure to serve as a roof.

As she began to look for matches in the few provisions the producers had given her, she heard the low rumble again. She realized it was an animal sound. And that there were no matches. She did find a small box labeled *Fire Starters*. She emptied the contents of the box: a steel tube with a metal stick in it, a small bottle labeled *Lighter Fluid* (*Lighter than what?* she wondered.), a piece of string, and instructions. She carefully read the instructions in the fading light. Finally, she poured the lighter fluid into the steel tube, threaded the string through the top of the metal stick, dipped it into the tube, and struck the strip of gritty metal on the outside of the tube.

Nothing happened.

She struck it again. Fire! She had made fire! She let out a whoop of excitement—which blew out the flame.

She repeated her fire-making process once again and carefully touched the fire to the sticks she had stacked in front of the shelter entrance earlier. It did not catch right away. She held the fire closer to the center and waited.

Nothing happened.

She didn't want to lose the flame, but she needed to look around for something that might help. She carried the lit metal matchstick around her campsite looking for…she had no idea what.

Finally, she dropped the flame. It caught on a small piece of dried grass. She quickly stamped out the fire so Smokey the Bear wouldn't show up.

Tears welled in her eyes as she realized she would have to light the match again. She lit it with slightly less effort and then realized the dry grass would help light her fire! She placed some dried grass on the stack of wood and lit it carefully. She was getting good at this.

With the fire blazing, she took off her hoodie and climbed into the small structure. A few hours later, she awoke to the low rumbling sound again. It was definitely closer.

She lay awake staring at the stars through the pine bough of her roof for what seemed like hours. She finally fell asleep again and didn't wake 'til the sunbeams forced her eyes open. She immediately began gathering long sticks to create a basis for a new roof.

During the last few days leading up to this adventure, she had watched video after video of people making wilderness shelters. She was very fond of the green grass and moss roofs many had used. She continued to gather and stack the sticks over the opening of her stone walls. She finally began digging just under thatches of grass and moss. She carefully carried each section and placed them on top of the sticks.

When she had finished, she looked at her handiwork: a masterpiece. After a quick meal of jerky and nuts, she climbed back into her shelter. She fell asleep thinking, *Just five more days*.

The rumbling woke her just before dawn.

In the hazy light, she saw a bit of a silhouette through a crack in the sticks. The grass on the roof moved. Zelinda froze in terror.

Again, the sound came, low and menacing. Bits of sticks and dirt began to rain down on her as what was clearly a wild animal began scratching at the roof. Zelinda felt a heavy weight on her legs. She was finally brave enough to reach a hand down.

She felt…fur.

Another noise reached her—this time it sounded more like a purr. She dared to look down toward her feet. There was a beautiful house cat lying on her legs, purring.

Over the next few days, Zelinda was sure she lost the last five pounds she had been struggling with. She became fast friends with the kitty. And, unbelievably (even to Zelinda), she won.

The satin sheets on the high-end designer bed in the high-end designer master bedroom of the high-end designer mansion could not have felt more comforting to Zelinda or her furry best friend. Zelinda stretched and thought, *Home!*

Karen Benckenstein was a nonprofit executive and fundraiser for a decade. She is now a freelance writer in addition to being a wife and mom to four teenagers. Karen writes about local people and organizations as well as ways to achieve wellness in mind, body, and spirit. She just finished her first novel, *Boundless*.

THREE
BULLET HOLES

BY EMILY BENTON

E very Saturday, there was a market at the end of the street called a *tianguis*. It was filled with fresh produce, a pound of blackberries for two dollars, a pound of strawberries for three. There were sweet tamales with the hottest green sauce sold by a leathered, hunched old man. He would reach down and grab them out of a metal pot the size of a toddler. I bought fresh-squeezed orange juice in a bag with a straw to sip along my path. It was the bright banner at the end of my week. I looked forward to it for the happy influx of calories, but more so I could look people in the eyes so we might smile at each other.

One time, a toothless lady told me I was the whitest person she had ever seen in her life and asked to touch my face. She came from an Indigenous group in the mountains. I knew she was telling the truth, because I was the only white person I saw for an entire year. (I did see an albino once; we waved at each other).

I was fighting off loneliness with the rush of new experiences, and it was working so far. This new world opened abruptly, and it never surprised me or anyone else that I would move to another country to be a green card bride. We met the usual way, in a beach town where my expat parents lived, and it all made sense at the time, even to them.

My soon-to-be husband lived in a part of Mexico that wasn't marketing to tourists. If they were, the tagline would be, "Watch your step! We've rolled severed heads onto a dance floor full of people!" instead of, "Come see our beaches, maybe snorkel a bit!"

I wasn't allowed to walk around alone at night, but during the day, everyone I ran into was cordial. They could see the pathetic desperation in my face to make a friend, clumsily start a conversation in my second language, or just laugh at something on the TV at the same time. I found a cool vegan restaurant, even though I was fine eating meat. I found a bright nail salon, and then one day, I found a job.

It was an English school run by a man having an affair with the secretary turned "executive assistant." I rolled my eyes when I found out, just like anyone would. It's almost too cliché to remember. She was beautiful but drenched with insecurity, obviously. He was tall, goofy, and reminded me of Inspector Clouseau, with a big bushy mustache, calculated crisp English, and a Volkswagen. I had to keep myself from pulling her aside multiple times a day to give her a girl-power pep talk. She was an adult, and I knew how good a lecture would land with me if I were her, so I had to internally drop it.

My students laughed at me, I was horrible at being "in charge," and teaching the *th* sound made everyone blush. Some days, I would have to find my way on the bus to a local school and I'd arrive ill-prepared and sweaty, but they still loved it, and so did I.

I did make one friend named Ari. She was one of the only people who treated me like a real friend, not like an outsider narc. I'm glad we became friends, because it turns out it wasn't a job at all. They closed down a few months later, and I never got paid. It was worth it, anyway. Isn't everything?

I didn't fully understand Mr. G.C.'s family. Of course I didn't. In-laws are hard enough; try it in another language! His birth dad lived in Ensenada, his stepdad played keyboards in a band, and his mom sold cosmetics. His two little brothers were irresponsible but harmless. They were normal, as much as that word matters, but his extended family had a lot more flare than a midnight piano cha-cha for tips or a new mascara.

He had an uncle who spoke pristine English. He stood like a metal rod was installed in his spine, shoulders back, chin up, Miss America posture. Never a wrinkle on any shirt, always the collected demeanor, but his natural intimidation outweighed all kindness. He looked me straight in the eyes a year prior and told me, "Don't get involved with my nephews."

I never did well with a firm demand, but turns out, I should have listened to him. Oh, the power of reverse psychology. He owned all kinds of properties, cars, and supported most of his family while his kids lived in the U.S. People respected him, feared him, and talked to him like they owed him one million dollars, and maybe, if they charmed him enough, he would forget about it. Turns out, he wasn't a forgetful person.

I remember driving around the city once with my green card recipient and his little brothers. I pointed and said, "What's that on the roof? All along the top of the building, do you see it?" They all laughed.

"Bullet holes. Someone tried to hide there a few months back. Never got out."

The white-painted cement was covered in polka dots of gunfire. What did I think it could be, a drainage system? An elaborate work of art? I thought I was street-smart until I moved there. They spoke casually about things I could never fathom in my previous life. They knew about the underbelly of the cartels because, as I'd soon discover, they were all a part of one.

I noticed a lot more bullet holes around town after that, and maybe that's why people smiled at me after all.

FOUR

WHEN PIGS FLY

LIL' BIRDY

W inny sat propped up on the living room sofa, her feet straight out in front of her, too short to even reach the edge. Winny felt very small sitting there alone. Although she had been on the sofa before, this was the first time she was by herself.

She looked around the room, focusing on the mint green floral wallpaper with the tiny little songbirds. She noticed that the sun was shining through the windows like spotlights on one bird in particular, a beautiful royal blue bird with long tail feathers covered in large white polka dots. Winny continued to watch in amazement as the sun's beam moved and made it look like the bird was flying,

Winny smiled. *I wish I could fly,* she thought. Winny tried to flap her ears like she had seen Dumbo do, but nothing happened.

Winny moved her eyes to look out the big picture window and

then to the large oak tree in the yard, where she saw a magnificent banana-yellow-bellied bird flying then landing on a small branch midway up the tree. Winny watched in wonder as the tiny bird flew out over the yard, stopping on the fence and then flying back to the tree. Over and over again it took off, flew around, then landed once again on the branch.

She tried to copy the bird, but just like before, nothing happened. Winny watched and watched the tiny bird, trying to mimic its every move, but nothing was working.

Winny wished she had an umbrella. After all, Mary Poppins used an umbrella to fly. Maybe that was all that she needed. Winny's birthday was next week, and right then and there, she decided that she would ask for an umbrella just her size. She practiced in her head all that she had seen Mary Poppins do and dozed off deep in thought.

Winny awoke to a small pecking sound coming from the living room window. There, to her delight, was the banana-yellow-bellied bird. It was wanting Winny to come out and play.

Oh, how Winny wanted to go, but she was stuck up on the sofa with no way to get down. Where was Christobell, and why had she left her all alone?

Winny cried, but there was no answer.

The house was quiet. She had been left behind. Winny thought Christobell loved her, but now she wasn't sure. Winny tried to recall the fun times they had spent together, the places they had gone, the things they had seen and experienced together, but something was different.

Something had changed. Something was wrong. What had happened to Christobell? Now Winny was not only sad and alone, Winny was sad, alone, and worried. Winny cried and cried until there were no more tears.

The house grew dark as the sun set behind the hills, and Winny had not moved an inch, eyes wide open and scared. She tried to think good thoughts, but they would always circle back to worry.

Then she tried counting sheep, but Winny could only count to ten, so that was not working either. Winny decided to play a game; after all, that was what Christobell would do.

Christobell loved playing games, her favorite being, "And now we will…" Christobell would say things like, "And now we will make the bed" or "And now we will go outside," and it was Winny who had to decide what would happen next.

Winny, in a loud, strong voice like Christobell would have done, announced, "And now we will fly!"

In her mind, Winny could see Christobell on the swing, getting higher and higher, and then, in a burst of energy, jumping from the swing seat in an attempt to fly.

No, that will not work, thought Winny. *I have seen Christobell come back down every time and fuss about her ankles tingling and burning. Hmm,* she thought.

It was then that Winny remembered the time Christobell climbed up on the roof of the oil shed.

It was rather blustery that day, and Christobell jumped, thinking she would fly, but no, she only tumbled and rolled. Christobell had tried over and over again until her body was sore and tired. Winny pleaded with her to try again—just one more time and she might fly.

Christobell agreed and quickly ran back into the house, leaving Winny behind with the dark storm clouds looming overhead. Moments later, when Christobell returned, she had her bed pillow tucked under her arm, and, looking up at the roof of the shed, she placed it on the ground in hopes that it would help cushion her fall.

Only if needed, of course.

Christobell once more climbed up the back of the oil shed and onto the roof. Looking at Winny, she gave her the thumbs-up sign, waited for a gust of wind, and jumped. It seemed like Christobell had finally done it—she flapped her arms, and it appeared she inched higher in the sky.

"I'm flying! I'm flying!" she cried with glee.

Suddenly the wind stopped, and Christobell fell quickly to the ground, right smack dab in the middle of the fluffy pillow. The pillow exploded, and feathers went sailing in every direction. It looked like big snowflakes, much like the ones Christobell and Winny would watch fall from the sky during the winter. They laughed until they heard loud and fast footsteps coming in their direction.

Mrs. Winchester then appeared and was not too happy with either of the girls for making such a mess and ruining such a fine and good pillow. "No dinner for you, and off to bed early."

Christobell hung her head and walked toward the back door to the house.

"Not so quick young lady," cried Mrs. Winchester. "You better take Winny with you." Mrs. Winchester then grabbed Winny very roughly and flung her in Christobell's general direction.

She landed on the ground with an *ouf!* She was frightened until Christobell picked her up. She hugged her and held her close, so close Winny could hardly breathe; she bent her head down and kissed the top of her head.

Any pain Winny had felt quickly diminished. Oh, how she loved the way Christobell's embrace felt, the way she would hold and rock her. She especially loved the little songs she would sing to her. She made her feel loved, alive, and wanted, and she drifted off to sleep.

Still half asleep, Winny heard a jingling sound followed by the creaking of a door and someone running in her direction. She froze and was so afraid until she saw Christobell running into the room, tears streaming down her face.

"She's here! She's here!" she cried, half laughing and half crying.

Christobell held Winny in her arms, and they swung back and forth. She kissed her and squeezed her and laughed as she held her out in front of her. She flung Winny up in the air and caught her. She did it again, and this time, Winny barely missed hitting the ceiling.

And then, grabbing Winny and placing her out in front of her, having a good hold on her, Christobell began turning in quick circles and spun her around the room a few times, and Winny laughed. She was flying! She was gliding like a bird through the air on a shaft of wind.

She was flying, really flying.

Christobell then pulled Winny in and hugged her, squeezing her again and again. Taking a seat on the couch, she rocked Winny and kissed her head...and said, "We left so early this morning, and when I woke up, I looked to find you, and you were not there. I cried and cried, thinking of you home and all alone." Another squeeze, another kiss, as Christobell cried tears of happiness.

Picking Winny up, Christobell walked out to the backyard and out to the swing, where she let Winny sit in her lap so they could swing together.

Winny came to realize that day that, as wonderful as flying was, and it was truly wonderful, being loved by Christobell was even more wonderful, and that feeling of truly being loved made her heart soar. Even the banana-yellow-bellied bird didn't have what she had.

Winny, a plump little pink velveteen piggy, was loved, bald patches with stuffing sticking out and all. Loved by a little girl who wanted and needed her.

Lil' Birdy migrated from the land of the Great Lakes to the eastern shores of the mighty Pacific. Seasons later, she traversed the mighty Rockies a time or two, where she enjoyed the high mountain elevations, fresh mountain air, and cool clean waters. There were also two enjoyable stops in the land of mini-pearls and Johnny Cash before she made her way to Texas.

Upon arriving in the great state, there was much to see, starting with the third coast, on to the hill country and heart of the state, before settling down on the caprock of the High Plains. A lover of shiny pens and leather journals, Lil' enjoys time in her garden, where she finds joy writing her stories and fairy tales, surrounded by her many bird and squirrel friends.

FIVE
A BROTHER'S GIFT

IRWIN BLACK

Daniel had always been jealous of his little brother, although they were close. They shared a friendship that most brothers never attained. For Kevin, good fortune had always walked beside him. Daniel struggled his whole life just to catch a break. He had stuck it out long enough to gain a manager position at the convenience store just down the street from Kevin's office. Every day, his little brother would come by to get a Coke and a candy bar. He would pull up in his cherry-red '69 Camaro, and Daniel would imagine himself cruising down the road with a gorgeous blonde sitting beside him.

One day, Kevin didn't come for his midday snack. As soon as Daniel got some free time, he called his mom. "Hey, I'm worried about Kevin. He didn't come by the store today."

"Oh, dear." His mom spoke apologetically. "I forgot to call you.

Kevin passed out at work today, and they rushed him to the ER. The doctor says it's his heart."

Daniel's spirits sank. *How could this happen to Kevin? Nothing bad ever happens to Kevin.* That day, Daniel put away all feelings of jealousy for his brother.

For months, Kevin was in and out of hospitals and clinics. They ran test after test, and Daniel spent all his free time with his little brother. "The doctors say you need a new heart."

"I know. I wish I could just call up the bank and they would send one over." Kevin tried to stay positive, but everyone knew the waiting list was long and the chances of finding a match were slim.

Daniel spent many nights with his brother. Watching him get weaker and weaker. He would watch Kevin sleep, and he would talk to himself; sometimes, he would talk to God. "Why is this happening? He doesn't deserve this kind of ending. Why isn't it me lying there? Lord, if there was something I could do, you know I would."

As Daniel was walking toward Kevin's room one day, his mom and the doctor met him in the hall. His mother looked him in the eyes, her eyes glistening in the dim light. "Doc says your brother only has a few days. Kevin asked to see you as soon as you got here."

Daniel hurried to the room. He fought to keep back the tears. Kevin's pale, fragile body lay there. Daniel thought back on the countless times he'd wished he could trade places with Kevin. Before, it was because he wanted all the success his brother was blessed with; now he just wanted his brother to live.

As he approached his bed, Kevin's eyelids cracked open, and a smile brightened his lips. He motioned for Daniel to lean in. "I need you to help me into my wheelchair and take me up to the roof. I need to show you something."

Daniel obliged, and soon, the two looked out over the city. The sunset cast a golden glow through the clouds. Daniel couldn't help but think how the sun was not only setting on the day but also on his brother's life.

Kevin gazed up at Daniel and looked deeply into his eyes. "I know life has dealt you some hard times, brother. I want to help you."

Surprise erupted on Daniel's face. "You want to help me?"

"Yes, Daniel, I want you to do me a favor. Look down at the parking lot."

Daniel peered over the side.

"What do you see?" Kevin motioned as if he were looking, too.

A sparkle lit in Daniel's eyes. "I see your car."

"No, you see *your* car." Kevin raised a weak hand. In it were the keys to his shiny red Camaro.

The tears that Daniel had fought back gushed forth. "I never wanted it to be like this. I'm so sorry I was ever jealous of you. Please forgive me."

"I forgive you, Daniel, and I want this to be a new start for you. I had a good life. Now it's your turn." With those words, Kevin closed his eyes.

After wheeling Kevin back to his room, Daniel had a long cry while holding his mom. He left the hospital knowing that he might not see his brother alive again.

Early the next morning, Kevin's room filled with the hustle and bustle of nurses and doctors running in and out. Kevin woke to see his mom's face, cheeks wet with tears, yet covered with joy he hadn't seen in months.

A nurse grabbed his arm and started taking his blood pressure.

A doctor bent over and began speaking. "Kevin, I'm Doctor Stephens. A donor heart has become available, and we are prepping you for surgery now."

Kevin was confused. *Is this real? Am I just dreaming?* "Mom. What is going on?"

Kevin's mom looked at him. Her face wore an expression he had never seen before. "Kevin, when Daniel left last night, he took the Camaro. On the way home, he was in a terrible accident. The doctor said he was a perfect match. They are giving you his heart."

Irwin Black was raised in a small town, but he's a country boy at heart. His first novel, *Silver and Blood*, is a fun tale pitting cowboys against vampires with a literary twist. It is available at your favorite retail location. For more information, visit www. irwinblack.com.

SIX
THE TRUTH IS ON THE ROOF

KIM BLACK

"You'll find the truth on the roof. And remember that I love you always."

Those were his final words to me before he drew his last breath. A long, labored breath that faded into a hiss. Then Dad was gone.

A strange cocktail of emotions sloshed through me. Relief that his pain was over. Honor that I was allowed to be at his side when he left. Sorrow that our occasional brief meetings had ended.

Dad had spent his life as an airline pilot, flying all over the world. Mother had instilled in me her acute phobia of flying. They were a match made somewhere just a little south of Heaven. Dad came home one weekend a month until Mother passed six years ago. It wasn't often enough, but it was what we had—except for my birthdays. For twenty-four years, Dad never missed a single birthday.

On my tenth birthday, he'd taken me to the rooftop café overlooking downtown. It was the highest I'd ever been. Twelve stories. Thrilling and terrifying at the same time.

He wore his navy suit and maroon tie. He had me dress up in my best dress, and he gave me a single pink rose. His deep brown eyes pinched in a never-ending smile. We sat at the corner table; it was the best they had. Mother couldn't stomach the view, so it was our special time together. That night. we had filet mignon and mashed potatoes followed by tiramisu.

"Only the very best for my princess," he'd said over and over. Dad then gave me a little blue box with a gold charm bracelet inside. From the first loop hung a golden rosebud. "This is just the first one." And he circled the bracelet around my wrist, securing the clasp as if he'd done it a million times.

"Thank you, Dad."

Once the server had cleared our table, Dad led me to the railing. I trembled a little, looking out over the buildings and the traffic toward the mountains in the distance. But Dad held my hand.

"Don't be scared." He nudged my chin with his knuckle. "I won't let anything happen to you."

I remember thinking that I could do anything or be anywhere if my dad was there. He'd protect me. I peered down without fear. I looked up and out without fear. The sky had turned a lovely purple, and the stars winked and blushed from a million miles away. I saw them, and for the first time in my life, I knew they saw me.

"Now, choose one petal from your rose." He let me pull off one circle of pink silky flesh. I held it up for him to inspect, and he bent down to kiss it. "Now you make a wish and kiss it, too."

I followed his instructions. I closed my eyes and wished. Maybe it was a silly wish for a ten-year-old girl, but I wanted nothing more than a brother. I'd always wanted a brother, but Mother said she couldn't have any more children and that I should be happy to be Daddy's princess. I was happy, but still, I wished. The starlight fluttered in my stomach, and I opened my eyes to my Dad's broad smile and pressed the petal to my pursed lips.

"All right, then." He gestured to the railing. "Toss it over."

I did. The little round of pink glowed in the twilight as it fell until a breeze swept it into the darkness. I took a deep, excited breath, but Dad held up one finger.

"Don't tell me your wish—or anyone else—or it won't come true."

So I kept that wish locked in my heart until my next birthday, when I wished for it again. Again and again, every year, I stood in the same place, holding Dad's hand, kissing the petal, and throwing it to the wind and stars. The same wish bubbled in my heart until it was no longer a wish but just a ritual. Simply the way I spent my birthday with my father.

You'll find the truth on the roof.

So many years later, I didn't have to wonder what he was talking about. I knew which roof. I knew when. My birthday was in three weeks.

My charm bracelet jangled at my wrist, heavy with gold butterflies, crowns, flowers, and even a sparkling diamond or two. I donned a pink dress and painted my nails to match. I made up my face three times for crying off my mascara twice. I could do this. I wasn't a fearful child anymore.

What did I think I would find? What was I looking for? He'd said I'd find the truth, but I had no idea what that meant. A letter from Dad's lawyer assured me that more information would follow.

"Happy birthday, Miss Morgan." The host greeted me as I stepped out of the elevator toward the café. He handed me a pink rose. "Your table is all prepared. Please follow me."

My stomach ached with each step I took. This was the first time I'd been on this roof without my father. Who would hold my hand? Who would help me send my wish to the stars?

As I neared the railing, I gazed out over the city and the mountains beyond, pushing down my fears. I searched up to the stars, hoping for an answer to my fears. I could see the corner of our table—my table, with a little blue box sitting at my place. Tears welled up, but I swallowed them back.

But as the host stepped aside, I froze in place. Opposite my chair stood my father, looking exactly as he had on my tenth birthday. Blue suit, dark-red tie, and flashing brown eyes.

I blinked away the illusion, but when I opened my eyes again, the illusion remained.

Another step, and my heart slammed in my chest. Dad held his hand out to me.

"Hello, Morgan."

But it wasn't Dad's voice—not quite. I stared into his eyes. Lighter brown than Dad's. He was younger—maybe only a dozen years older than me. And his shoulders were slimmer.

"Hello?" My voice trembled. My body trembled. The rose trembled.

"Please sit down." He circled the table, nodded away our host, and pulled out my chair. He waited for me to settle and took several deep breaths before he took his place across the table.

All I could do was stare. He was my father, but not. I was overwhelmed with a sudden flash of recognition. Deep inside, my heart knew this man. I knew who he was. A thousand questions were answered before he said a word.

Why only one weekend a month? Why was my birthday so special to him? I knew these answers and so many more. My father had a second family. A secret. And that secret was me. I wasn't afraid anymore.

You'll find the truth on the roof.

He tugged at his tie and then gulped a hard swallow of water. "I know this will be difficult to understand, but I'm—"

I glanced at my rose as a petal shook free and fell upon the little blue box in front of me. "You're my brother."

Kim Black is a not-quite-cozy author of several novels of multiple genres. For more information, visit www.kimblackink.com.

SEVEN
THE YOUNGER SISTER

N. K. BRIGHT

My younger sister is what she calls me. Never by my name.

"This is my younger sister. The one that died," she says as people glance at me with a wary look on their faces. And then, behind her hand, Sis leans closer, like she's sharing a huge secret. "She saw the afterlife."

It is true that I almost died in a horrible car wreck on a wet, slippery mountain road during a late spring storm. I remained in a medically induced coma for over a week so that my bruised and broken body could heal.

Honestly, I don't remember much about that entire first month of recovery. I faded in and out of consciousness, my waking moments tolerable only with the use of intense pain medication. They say you can become an addict to the buzz, but I did not care.

I just wanted the world to go away. The truth is, it's the afterlife part that remains foggy, despite what my sister tells everyone.

There is one constant comfort that I do remember during those questionable days of whether I might live or die. A soft voice of reassurance and mumbled prayers. When I finally opened my eyes, he was there. The hospital chaplain. The nurses told me after I woke up from the coma that he had visited me several times a day. As I began to gain consciousness, he was there offering a sip of cold liquid or a chip of ice.

One day, he brought me a vanilla frozen yogurt. "Vanessa. God loves you," he whispered as he spooned the cold treat into my mouth. "You still have a purpose on this earth."

Me, with a purpose? I highly doubted that, but I had never tasted anything so good. The creamy texture paired with the cold against my tongue reminded me of the simple pleasures in life.

During the second month of my hospitalization, I became more and more alert and aware of my surroundings. My heart fluttered whenever he leaned closer. The sterile surroundings seemed even more isolating when he wasn't there. In my muddled brain, I assumed his only purpose was to administer last rites. Maybe ease the burden for my sister because she was so distraught. As I began to think more clearly, I could not remember her being by my bedside.

We began having conversations, my hospital chaplain and me. Nothing of much importance at first, and my words came out scratchy and strange because of the tubes that had been in my throat. He was the first one to wheel me out of the ICU to the picture window. As I looked out from the third floor onto a world alive and vibrant, I could not recall the world having that many different shades of green.

"It's beautiful," I said.

"Yes, you are," he replied. And then he whispered, "I love you."

I wasn't surprised.

Our conversations became more intimate after that day. We discussed our past, and we planned our future. He taught me so many things about life, learning to trust, and the love of our Lord. I warned him about my sister, and he would talk to me about forgiveness.

"Will you be my boyfriend?" I asked him.

"I will," he said.

While the doctors worked to heal my body, my boyfriend worked to heal my heart and soul.

My sister was busy planning my future, too, and my introduction back into a normal life. She had big plans, all right. Her intentions had nothing to do with her concern for me.

The whole con was her idea.

I should have figured out what she was planning on the day she told me, "These afterlife stories are making big news. This young girl got a movie deal!" She said this from behind a newspaper, which she then folded under her arm before leaving without saying goodbye.

I told my chaplain that she was up to something. That it most assuredly involved me, and that I wouldn't like it. I told him I was scared. "You don't realize what she is capable of," I said.

"I am part of your life now," he told me. "There is nothing to worry about. If you feel uncomfortable talking about the wreck, then we will explain that to your sister."

He would never understand. My older sister has manipulated me for as long as I can remember. Every minute of every day is filled with her presence. My parents never intervened because she was the perfect daughter. The perfect loving sister who wanted nothing more than my happiness. The perfect charlatan disguised as a tender-hearted beauty.

In high school, she screened my friends. Forget about boyfriends. Her list of unacceptable traits was endless. She found something wrong with every boy who showed the slightest bit of interest in me. His hair is too long. His mother was married before. His father is a garbage truck driver, although this was the one who gave me my first kiss. I really liked him, and his parents were wonderful people.

My destiny was to live under the shadow of my older sister. The true severity of the situation hit me during the summer after I graduated high school. My parents moved us both out of their house into an apartment. Sis already had my registration approved and my fall class schedule at the local community college. No one had asked me where I wanted to go to college or what I wanted to major in.

By then, I was too weary to argue. It was easier to go along with her. Although college did allow me some freedom. I got really good at hiding in the library or hanging out in a classmate's dorm room. These little bits of peace away from her had been worth the verbal lashings later.

With heels clicking on the tiled floor, Sis marched into my hospital room one day. The scent of her perfume assaulted my nose. I kept my eyes closed, but she tapped me on the shoulder.

"Do you remember anything about those days you were in a coma?" Sis asked.

"Not really," I said. "It's all still fuzzy."

"Try to remember. Did you have any visions? Did you see faces, maybe the faces of Granny and Grandpa?"

"They've been dead over twenty years. Why would I see their faces?" A small churn of annoyance tickled my stomach. This happens when my sister's about to make me do something I don't want to do.

"Try to remember for me, okay?" She leaned over the bed and gently kissed my cheek, something that had never happened in my entire life. There has never been any type of sisterly affection between us. I faked exhaustion and closed my eyes.

A few days later, Sis stormed into my room again to see my boyfriend and me holding hands, our foreheads touching. I can't remember what he whispered because I was focused on the love reflected in his eyes, which was why I hadn't noticed the clicking of her heels in the hall.

She dismissed him immediately. "I need to talk to my younger sister in private." The words 'in private' were spit out of her mouth with vile authority. The rant that followed lasted a full thirty minutes after he left. I know this, because I stared at the clock on the wall above her head.

"What are you thinking? He is a hospital chaplain who probably only makes twenty-thousand dollars a year, if that much. He could never provide for you. You would never have anything. Your life would be miserable. He will never be anyone of importance."

"He is important to me," I said. "We have each other. That's all we need, and I love him." I couldn't believe those words had come from my mouth. To defy my older sister was not tolerated.

Her beautiful face turned purple with rage, and her eyes shaded to black with hate. She slapped my cheek, spun on her three-inch heels, and left.

The next time she visited, she brought a man with her. "He is going to help us write about your experience in the afterlife." He was thin with mousy brown hair and wire-rimmed glasses, and his hand felt clammy and soft when he shook mine. If she said his name, I never heard it.

He peered at me over his glasses. "Tell me what Heaven looked like."

"I went to Heaven?" I mumbled. My head was groggy. Physical therapy had taken a lot out of me that morning, and the pain meds were finally kicking in.

I wanted to ask him to leave, but no sound came from my lips. I gave in to the pain and prayed that my boyfriend would come to my rescue.

Sis brought the man to my room every day for the next two weeks. They talked about my visit to the afterlife while I lay in a fuzzy-headed state. My arms and limbs felt heavy, I lost my appetite, and I became discouraged. It seemed that only a few days ago, I was making good progress. I don't remember exactly at what point I believed, but I had most assuredly gone to the afterlife and walked through a green pasture. Maybe it was Heaven.

My boyfriend never visited me again. I didn't know what Sis did or said, but I felt certain his job was on the line and his reputation at stake because of her lies.

The nurse brought me breakfast one morning and announced the big news. "You are being released tomorrow."

To say I was surprised is an understatement.

Sis made a big deal of bringing a new outfit for me to wear. Helping me into my clothes, she seemed unusually jovial. "This is a great day. You can help so many people."

As we drove off, I stared at the reflection of the clouds and trees in the glass building. The building that had been my home for two months. The place where he worked. The place where my faith was strengthened. The place I fell in love.

The next six months were a whirlwind of talks, shaking hands, and book signings. Oh, yes, there was a book. Sis had overseen every step of the process to publication. How we had a book in hand that fast, I'll never understand. Her name appeared first on the cover, and my name was preceded by "with" in a tiny font at the bottom.

I really didn't have much to say during interviews, as Sis did most of the talking. I was recovering from a horrific accident, after all, and people had great sympathy for what I had endured. Book sales went through the roof, and people were very generous with their cash donations to help our ministry.

My older sister was on cloud nine. She loved managing our little enterprise.

"I booked you on television," she said one morning over coffee. I focused my attention on two hummingbirds' flit and flutter around the feeder, thinking about the wonder of God's world. A bird's song. The view from a mountaintop. The beauty He bestows on us and that surrounds us every day. The simple pleasures sometimes make life bearable. My heart still ached, though, for tender kisses and a comforting touch, but I tried to find purpose.

"Television?" I squeaked as I choked on my coffee.

"Yes, the local morning show. It's nothing to be concerned about. You'll sail right through."

After that interview, Sis reported record book sales. We'd hit several bestseller lists, and requests for appearances were pouring in, which brought her even closer to her goal of negotiating a movie deal. While she checked stats on the computer, I poured a half gallon of milk down the drain and then told her I had to go get more.

Which brings me to why I find myself sitting on the roof of our childhood home staring at the stars. The for-sale sign in the yard brought tears to my eyes when I walked past it. Sis says we have too many medical bills to pay, but I never gave her my key to this house.

When I was little, I had spent a lot of time sitting on our roof. My window nestled neatly under a small dormer that faced the street. Sis's window faced the backyard.

This is the one place I could find peace and escape from her interference. I could breathe. I could hear my own thoughts without her voice in my head. The rough bricks against my back felt solid as I had watched the world from my perch. There is something comforting about the dark.

My thoughts drift to that cold day when that spring storm changed my life. I remember clearly that the guard rail had been new and shiny. Was it the icy road? Had I intentionally turned my wheels to that cliff? Maybe. Perhaps I had taken control and made a decision. What had been going on in my head that day still haunts me. I may never remember.

I watch car lights approach slowly, bob up and down over a bump, and then surprisingly turn into the drive. The vehicle rolls to a stop behind my car, and my boyfriend gets out.

"Hi," he says.

"Hi," I say, although my voice does not reflect the erratic pounding of my heart.

He walks into the yard and looks up. "I've missed you."

"I know," I say. I don't have the courage to tell him how achingly much I have missed him. There are no words. A sob catches in my throat.

"Wait right there, I forgot something." He spins around and hurries back to his car. When he emerges again, he holds two cups with handles sticking out of the top.

"Yogurt."

I smile.

"Can I join you?"

I nod yes, but I am terrified.

"Was that a nod? Because it's dark, and I can't be sure."

"Yes." This is much harder than standing on the edge of a cliff.

As he scrambles out of the window onto the roof, I reach for the treats and hold them both until he sits down.

"She requested an increase in your pain meds, and then your sister threatened to sue the medical center unless I stayed away."

He knew what I was thinking.

"That explains my fuzzy head just before they released me." We sit in silence as I focus on the sweet cold against my tongue. "How did you know where to find me?" I ask.

"I remember everything we talked about."

"What if I had not been here?"

"Then I eat both yogurts and try again the next night."

I giggle.

"We should get married." He presses his shoulder against mine.

"I know of a great house for sale."

"Is it affordable?" he asks.

"It has a solid roof."

Natalie Cline Bright is an author, blogger, and speaker. Her stories and articles have appeared in numerous publications. She holds a BBA from WTAMU, enjoys talking to all ages about writing, and is the author of a middle-grade mystery series, a picture book series about rescue animals, and writes western romance for CKN/Wolfpack Publishing. Natalie is the author of two cookbooks with a focus on the history and food of chuck wagons and cow towns. She blogs about the people, places, and fascinating history of the Texas Panhandle at Prairie Purview. Sign up for her newsletter at https://nataliebright.com/.

EIGHT

LOST IN THE NIGHT

JOHN BROCK

The aroma of freshly brewed coffee led Griffin down the hallway into the common room. The early morning hours had passed slowly, and a shot of caffeine was exactly what he needed to get him through the rest of his shift. He walked briskly past the nurse's station, where Mrs. Brennan studied her computer.

"Please slow down," the charge nurse said without taking her eyes off the screen.

Griffin smiled and returned to his normal walk, feeling as if he were back in grade school. His first night working at Howell Nursing Home had taken a physical toll. Most nights, he had no trouble staying awake 'til the break of dawn, playing video games or hanging out with friends, but working the early morning hours had taken a physical toll he hadn't expected. Though he needed to save some money for his upcoming college expenses, Griffin was unsure he could make it to the end of summer.

When he reached the common-room entrance, three residents were seated at a table in the middle of the room, cradling steaming cups of coffee. It was only a bit after four in the morning, but all three men were wide awake, looking at Griffin curiously.

"Good morning," Griffin said. "I hoped I could grab a cup of coffee."

"Morning," one of the men replied with a deep, gruff voice. "And please, sit down with us a bit."

"I'm not sure Mrs. Brennan would like that," Griffin said. He walked over to the coffee maker on the counter, pulled out a Styrofoam cup from the stack by the sink, and poured himself a cup.

"Nonsense," the man with the deep voice replied. "Consider it one of your new job duties."

"Engaging with the residents," a small man with reading glasses replied.

"If Mrs. Brennan says anything, we'll stick up for you," the third man said. Unlike his friends, who were nearly bald, he had thick locks of grey hair that reached his shoulders. "Besides, we could use another player."

"Can't really play dominoes with three," the man with the reading glasses on replied. "Please, have a seat."

Griffin gave a look at the entryway, hoping Mrs. Brennan or another nurse wasn't watching, and walked over to the table. He pulled out a chair and joined the three men.

"My name's Roger," the man with the deep voice said, offering his hand.

Griffin shook it. "Griffin."

The other two men, Claude and Mike, introduced themselves as well. Adjusting his glasses, Claude walked over to the bookshelf and took down a box of dominoes.

"Blame Mike if you don't like the coffee," Claude said as he set the box in the center of the table.

Griffin took a sip, finding the coffee so strong he almost coughed, but he smiled instead. "It's very good."

"Our young man has taste," Mike said. "My friends here love to complain about it."

Claude shrugged his shoulders. "Just busting your chops."

Roger opened the box, and the three friends picked up the white tiles and placed them on the table. "We forgot to ask if you played."

"We're so old, we just assume everyone knows dominoes," Mike said with a wink.

"Not really, but I'm a fast learner."

"Good," Roger said as he scrambled the tiles with both hands. The clinking of the dominos felt somehow comforting, almost like wind chimes on a breezy spring day. "We'll play a practice round, show you the rules and strategy."

"If we can learn how to play," Claude said. "Anyone can."

Griffin followed their lead, each taking seven tiles and standing them with the black dots in front of him but hidden from the others. Mike set the first tile down, one with three dots on one half and one dot on the other.

"Now you can play of the three or the one," Roger explained.

Griffin studied his tiles, picking one that had three and five dots. He placed the three against Mike's three, leaving the one and five dots open to play. Claude studied his hand, placing a one-dot tile against the other, and the game moved along. It seemed simple enough, but when Griffin couldn't find a tile to play, they explained that he would pick one from the draw pile until he was able to play it. They went around the table several times until Mike ran out of tiles in his hand.

"Winner winner, chicken dinner," Mike called out.

"We don't usually play for points," Roger explained, laying down his tiles. "But this is how you tally them."

It seemed simple enough once the basic instructions were given. They played a few more games, with Griffin winning the second round.

"You're already a better player than Mike here," Claude said.

"Or Whitlock," Mike replied.

"Especially good old Whit," Roger said. "Dominoes wasn't his strong suit."

"Great poker player, though," Claude added. "I don't know how many pennies he won off me through the years."

Even though it was his first night, the name registered with Griffin. Earlier in the evening, he'd assisted a nurse with a resident in room 127. The man appeared thin and frail, his eyes vacant, and as Griffin helped him into his wheelchair for a bathroom break, the nurse explained that the resident was in the first stage of Alzheimer's and would be transferred to a hospice center within the next few days. Not an overtly religious person, Griffin had noted his last name on the room plaque and offered a silent prayer.

"Have you met Whitlock?" Roger asked, almost as if he read Griffin's thoughts.

"Yes," Griffin said, looking down at the table.

"He's gone, isn't he?" Claude said. "Not dead, of course. I mean, there's nobody home, right?"

"I don't think I'm really qualified to say."

"Come on, Griffin," Mike said. "You're as qualified as any of the quacks who work here."

Griffin gathered the courage to answer. "Claude is right. There's no light left in him that I could tell."

Roger shook his head. "I knew when Margaret passed, it was only a matter of time."

"Old Whit was a fighter, though," Mike said. "I believe he's still there, somewhere deep inside."

Roger stood and walked over to the coffee maker, picking up the carafe. He walked around the table, refilling everyone's cup, before returning it back to the warmer.

"There was something special about Whit and his wife," Roger explained. "Almost as if they were one person. Whitlock's been here, what, four years?"

"Five," Claude said.

"That's right," Mike said. "I got here right after he did."

"When Whit was diagnosed, it put Margaret in a tough place. Their two daughters lived in different parts of the country, and she couldn't take care of him alone."

"She never forgave herself," Claude added. "But everyone knew she did the right thing. Especially Whit."

"Margaret visited every day," Mike said. "Sometimes staying overnight. It was hard to remember she wasn't one of our fellow residents. I've been married and divorced a few times, and as much as I want to not believe in true love, they made it hard. Very hard."

The group grew silent, as if each hoped the other one would be brave enough to continue the story. Finally, Roger took a sip of coffee and cleared his throat.

"It was the saddest thing," Roger began. "Remember when everything went into lockdown during the pandemic?"

"Sure," Griffin said. "I spent my junior year taking online classes. Can't say I learned much that year."

"It was a nightmare around here," Claude said. "They kept us locked up like we were in prison and didn't allow visitors. At least once a week, an ambulance would show up to take another resident to the hospital. Some came back, and some didn't."

Taking a deep breath, Mike turned and looked directly into Griffin's eyes. "They don't allow smoking here, but Whit used to sneak up to the roof to smoke his cigarettes. They have cameras down every hallway, the nurses knew what he was doing, but Whit thought he was getting away with something."

"As long as he smoked outside," Claude said. "The nurses didn't care."

"They might have regretted that if anything ever happened to him," Roger added. "Family could've sued the pants off this place if he stumbled over the ledge or a sudden gust of wind pushed him off."

"Now, this was the old, strong Whit," Claude said. "He could take care of himself."

"When the lockdowns started," Roger said. "I noticed that Whit started taking his smoke break at the same time every day. Well, I got curious, so I started to peek out my window and see if anything funny was going on. One day, this old model Buick pulls up to the curb and parks. This lady wearing one of those surgical masks we all had to wear back then looks up at the roof for several moments and offers a pleasant wave. I realize that it's Margaret, and they've worked out this routine where she drives over every day to visit Whit up there."

"Roger told us what was going on," Mike said. "So every afternoon, we'd gather in the common room, open the blinds, and watch as the Buick parks and Margaret steps out. Even the nurses started to pull up a chair to watch. It was such a lovely thing."

"And then," Claude said, adjusting his glasses. "The Buick stops showing up."

Roger turned to the common room window, staring through the blinds at the dark night. "It all happened so fast. Margaret caught the virus, and in a matter of days, they are putting her in the ground. From that point on, old Whit just gave up. He's not showing up for our morning coffee, he's staying in his room for days on end. Mrs. Brennan tells us his disease is progressing at a rapid pace."

"Last time I spoke with him," Mike said, "it was as if I were talking to another person. Like he was lost in a maze, and he couldn't find a way out."

The group grew silent as more residents made their way into the room. An hour or so had passed, and Griffin knew it was time to help the kitchen staff get ready for breakfast. The three men told him he was welcome back anytime for a game, and Griffin thanked them as he threw his empty cup into the trash.

After taking down chairs off the tables in the cafeteria and helping roll up the silverware, Griffin took several cans of trash out to the dumpster. The rays of the morning sun lit up the sky as birds began to chirp and sing from the trees. After breakfast, his work shift would be over, but the beauty of the new day sparked an idea Griffin wanted to share with Mrs. Brennan.

The charge nurse was in an intense discussion with one of the nurses as Griffin approached the station. He thought of turning back, of bringing up the idea another day, but he knew his window of opportunity was closing. He waited patiently until the nurse walked away and Mrs. Brennan turned to him.

"What can I help you with, Griffin?" Her tone wasn't rude but harried.

It took a moment for him to gather the courage to speak, but when he did, he explained the plan in the most simple and direct way he could manage. Mrs. Brennan's face showed no emotion when he finished.

"What do you think?" he asked to break the awkward silence.

"I think it's brilliant," the charge nurse replied with a wink before returning to her computer.

Breakfast started at seven, and by six thirty, residents started to leave their rooms and head to the common room, filling it with talk and banter. Griffin helped the nurses gather the residents into a line along the hallway that led to the cafeteria. At seven, the line began to move, and Griffin and the nurses walked along the hallway to make sure it moved at a steady pace. Roger, Claude, and Mike were near the end of the line and wished Griffin a good day and that they hoped they would see him again tomorrow.

When the last resident entered the cafeteria and grabbed their empty tray, Griffin excused himself from the other nurses and headed back to the station. Mrs. Brennan and a young nurse were waiting for him, the charge nurse explaining it would be best if someone accompanied him and Mr. Whitlock just in case something happened.

The young nurse introduced herself as Nancy as they walked together to room 127. Mr. Whitlock was lying in bed, his empty tray at his bedside after he'd been fed. Nancy grabbed the wheelchair, pushed it over to the side, and put on the wheel brakes, and together they both lifted Mr. Whitlock out of bed and into the wheelchair.

"It's a beautiful day, Mr. Whitlock," Nancy said. "Griffin here thought it would be a good idea to get some fresh air."

The elderly man showed no sign of recognition. Griffin bent down and undid the wheel brakes and gently pushed the wheelchair toward the door. With most of the residents having breakfast, the hallway was mostly empty. They took a right turn toward the kitchen and weaved through the workers and metal sinks and ovens over to the service elevator. Nancy pressed the button, and the doors opened.

"You know this route pretty well, don't you?" Nancy said to Mr. Whitlock as the doors closed, but he merely stared ahead, as if he were in another world.

The elevator rumbled its way to the top floor, stopping with a jolt. When the doors opened, Griffin pushed the wheelchair onto the ramp that led up to the roof. As they neared the end of the ramp, the majestic morning sky came into view. An intense orange hue hovered on the horizon, sending streaks of light into the dark-blue sky. A few puffy clouds danced in the air with the promise of a beautiful summer day.

Griffin pushed the wheelchair to the brick ledge of the roof. The building was only four stories tall but located in a part of town that gave them an unobstructed view of the sky. He put on the wheel brakes again and looked down at Mr. Whitlock. Griffin hoped the scenery would bring back pleasant memories, and he studied the man's face for any hint of recognition, but Mr. Whitlock only stared straight ahead with eyes that seemed empty. For several minutes, they watched the morning sun rise. Nancy took a glance at her watch and told them it was time to go back inside.

It wasn't until Griffin had unlocked the brakes that he noticed Mr. Whitlock's right hand raised in a silent wave to the sun.

NINE
ROOFTOP IN HAVANA

BOKERAH BRUMLEY

V*iñales Valley*
      Sierra de los Órganos, Cuba

"Do you hear me?" The tobacco farmer never called young Abeo by his name. "*Salir de la carretera,*" the gruff voice demanded. "Get out of the way. Only fools are out walking in this storm. Not much under your rooftop. Is there?"

Abeo glanced upward to the poncho-topped man seated in the small cart without answering. Rain had been pounding the rooftops for days, but the storms meant his beloved Oya was nearby. But Abeo wasn't worth much after all—only a fool, perpetually in love with Oya's rain on his skin. Explaining it all to the farmer wouldn't help, so Abeo stepped off the stone thoroughfare into the flooded ditch.

The oxen tossed their horned heads, irritated by the usual October deluge which had slicked and soaked everything in the valley. The old man nodded once before he issued a sharp whistle that set eight bovine hooves plodding once more.

After the farmer passed, Abeo stepped back into the road. He bent down, shielding his face from the after-the-hurricane wind, which whipped the coconut trees side to side, but he wouldn't return to the barn until the drizzle stopped.

Twenty days until tourist season and his work in the hospitality villas.

Twenty days until Abeo could not secretly visit Oya in the curing barns.

And then one hundred and twenty nights without her. He had counted the days for two wet seasons as a grown man now. Abeo did not relish the upcoming return to the dryness and the city for visiting tourists. Oya made his wet season work on the tobacco farms bearable.

The dry season meant many things for their world. Fat men in suits would come buy their cigars, ogle his little sisters, and use his mother like the soul-emptied creatures they were.

In the courtyard of their home in the city, visitors rang the ship bell, warning his mother to make ready. She would hurry him and his sisters out of the one-room home. She made enough money each season to feed his sisters for the following year. But she couldn't hide the limping, the black eyes, the hard-to-move mornings after. Not from him. Not anymore.

And he planned to free her from the life she believed she must live to survive.

Abeo pulled his collar closer, his clothes already soaked

through. Overhead, the clouds thinned. He caught winks of the starlight world beyond. This storm would break soon. Oya could do as she wished with him. Abeo wished only to rescue his mother and save his sisters from his mother's life, and he would soon make his request.

When Oya next arrived, calling his name, wrapped in the Cuban winds, he would offer his entreaty. If he pleased her, perhaps she would grant his petition.

"Abeo."

The rumble woke him in his barn-floor bed of straw and burlap. "I am here," Abeo growled through gritted teeth, the fire in his belly already stoked by dreams of the powerful goddess. They weren't his memories, but they plagued him.

A black-eyed bee hummingbird zipped between the tobacco racks, wings a blur. Only two inches long, the iridescent pink head feathers shimmered in the moonlight. It settled on a rooftop crossbeam, tilting its head this way and that.

Abeo sat upright. "Oya? Are you there, in the roof?"

She never manifested as the same creature twice, but her laughter always began as thunderous sounds, echoing off the mountains, shrinking until it became the honeyed sounds from her human form.

Abeo blinked. Instead of the tiny bird, Oya stood before him, head thrown back, draped in ceremonial fabrics which swirled and stormed around her, a whirlwind dress and matching head wrap.

"Oya," he murmured.

She leaned against the drying racks. "I am here, son of the

Niger," she said, breathless from mirth. "I have missed you since the last storm."

"I have missed you."

Her pulse throbbed just above her collarbone, and the image brought other nights, other sounds to Abeo's mind. Heat surged through his veins again, but he did not speak.

"Son of the Yorùbá, son of my people," she murmured, as she always did, before acknowledging the tension wound tight within him. She held out her hands and motioned him nearer.

For the first time since she had taken Abeo as her companion, he hesitated, swaying from foot to foot. "I am not worthy, Orisha Oya," he began in formal tones and kneeled. "You may wish to choose another to entertain you."

Her gaze narrowed, and purple lightning flashed in her irises. "You have a request?"

Abeo moved to stand but reconsidered midway and resettled in a crouch instead. He bowed his head, watching from his periphery. "I have a petition."

She raised an eyebrow, but her expression softened. "I'm the water to quench your fire, Abeo, as you are mine." She smiled, a rainbow after a storm. "You please me as Shango did long ago." She tapped her chin. "I will listen, we will bargain, and soon, you will remember."

Havana, Cuba
  Three Weeks Later

The bell rang in the courtyard.

Abeo could hear the waves lap against the docks, knocking the boats together, down at Playa Baracoa. When he was a boy, when the noises in the bedroom were too much for him, he would run to the wharf to let his tears mix with the saltwater spray.

Then the twins came. And he would not allow himself to run away anymore.

The whistle of a train leaving La Coubre Station interrupted his thoughts. Abeo glanced over his shoulder, his hands clenched at his sides as he watched a man climb the steps and knock on the door beneath the stucco arch, a yearly tradition for so many men.

His mother's "friend"—he thought the word with a sneer—from the Tropicana cabaret always sent work. From Abeo's hiding place behind the trash cans, he could watch his sisters standing next to each other on the stoop. They both had their fingers pressed into their ears. This was the way they had grown up, his mother's attempt to protect them.

Back in the curing barn, under the tobacco hanging from the rooftops, Oya had been pleased with the appeal on behalf of his mother and sisters. She had agreed to come to the rescue on this day, and a storm stirred over the capital city—the last of the season.

"An interesting turn," Oya whispered as she stroked his cheek in the tobacco-drying barns. Then she twirled, morphed from woman to hummingbird, and disappeared. He hadn't seen her since.

Abeo strolled out from behind the trash and mounted the stairs two at a time. Oya would be here soon. She would burst in to save the day, as she had saved him, as he had saved her from her loneliness.

His sisters' eyes widened when they saw him, their smiles brightened. But he heard knuckles on flesh, heard his mother's muted wail. The neighbor's television blared to cover the noise. Always easier to ignore what didn't concern her, the neighbor said.

Abeo could not wait for Oya. He would confront the attacker man-to-man, face-to-face.

With a roar, Abeo kicked in the door. The slats splintered, and wooden shrapnel exploded across the barren room. Naked, his mother cursed. The scum fumbled with his pants, grunting still from the passion of drawing blood.

His mother's blood.

Red coursed down her chin.

Abeo roared. He was the god of thunder. He was the god of justice.

He drew winds down from the heavens to howl through the courtyard.

Lightning struck the palms outside.

Oya was coming. His mate was coming. She would dance on the rooftop and help him tear this evil apart.

The sky turned black overhead; the window glass darkened.

He advanced on the man who had fallen to his knees before him, hands clasped in a begging prayer.

An ox lowed outside. The out-of-place sound broke through the sounds of the tempest building above them. Puzzled, Abeo glanced over his shoulder, but when he looked back, the man had gone.

Instead, Oya stood before him. "I have searched for you since I returned from our ancestors, but you did not remember."

Abeo lowered his hands, the heat of his anger doused by the splash of her words in his heart. He lowered his chin in deference to the deity before him.

"You!"

Abeo spun toward his mother's breaking voice. Now covered, she sagged against the bed frame, staring at Oya.

"You," she repeated. With unsteady hands, she pressed her fingers over her lips. A tremble rolled through her. She staggered back, crumpling to the floor.

Abeo rushed forward, but Oya reached her first. Oya eased the woman into the bed and waved her hands over her. "She will wake soon. I have healed the broken." Oya dragged a chair close to the bed. "She will explain to you when she wakes."

Abeo ushered the twins inside, soothed their fears, and fed them their midday meal. When his mother finally stirred, he was there with a bowl of broth, but she waved him away from her bedside.

Then her gaze fell on Oya. "You," she said again.

"Me," Oya agreed.

The mother crossed her arms. "I took care of him as you asked."

Oya hugged herself. "You did."

"Is he what you believed he would become?"

"He called for the storm, and the storm listened." Oya beamed at the no-longer bruised woman. "He is Shango reborn, and soon, we will live together in the thunder and make the clouds our home."

Abeo cleared his throat. "You two make no sense."

Oya laughed but without thunder. "My love."

His mother reached for Abeo, pulling him close. She kissed his forehead. "At Orisha Oya's request, I came to Havana to protect you. I nursed you. I cared for you as my own," she placed Abeo's hand in Oya's, "waiting for her return."

Abeo studied the goddess who had filled his mind for months. She could be his. He could be hers, but his mother and sisters…

Oya stroked his palm. "Don't fear, Abeo. I'll send blessings on your mother, protectors for your sisters, until you're strong enough to strike fear in their hearts."

The truth echoed within Abeo, and he understood where his memories had come from and why Oya had never been far from his side. Across the Atlantic, thunder drums called his name, rattling the rafters as rain fell on the rooftop overhead.

And Shango turned to answer.

Bokerah Brumley lives on ten permaculture acres, complete with sheep, goats, peacocks, turkeys, geese, guineas, ducks, chickens, five home-educated children, and one husband.

TEN
LET'S CELEBRATE THE RAINY DAY

FRANKA DANIEL

Let's dance up on the rooftops like they were piano keys
Pet a gargoyle, hug a chimney, watch a flock of geese
Let's celebrate each day and night, laugh and sing
out loud
Let Thor and lightning guide us when the moon's behind a
cloud

Let's dance along the beach 'til there's ripples on the seas
Let's not reach out with a fist when we ask for peace
Let's paint the earth with smiles and the air with frankincense
Let's open all the windows and let's tear down the last fence

The skies will change from black to blue and then to black again

The sun will melt our trail of frozen tears
Hold my hand, don't let me fall off the face of this old world
Where eternity is only a few years

Let's celebrate the rainy day with old songs and absinthe
    Look straight into that morning sun and play tag with
the wind
    And when our purpose passes, there might be a better place
    Let's not leave before we know we put a smile on someone's
face

The skies will turn from black to blue…

ELEVEN
SANTA IS ON THE ROOF

SANDY HANEY

Many of us have childhood memories of hearing about Santa's magical leap into our chimneys to deliver Christmas presents. For those of us who had no chimney, we puzzled over how Santa would make his way inside our home with gifts in tow. I grew up by the ocean, where the average temperature is 75 degrees throughout the year. There was little need for fireplaces in that environment. Thus, I concluded that the hefty toy-maker descended from our attic.

The faded pink lead-based paint so commonly used in houses built in 1940 chipped each time we moved aside the board covering the attic's opening, but I wouldn't know of the paint's health risk until I had kids of my own. A ladder was brought in so we could climb up, hoist ourselves up into the dark storage room, and find some relic to satisfy our decorating pleasure.

I pondered what a chore it would be for Santa, but I knew if anyone was up to the challenge, it was him. The matter was settled. I would stay awake all night Christmas Eve so I could verify that Santa indeed descended through the attic to bring us presents.

When Christmas Eve came, I gathered pillows and blankets and stacked them on the old davenport, from which I would have the best view of the attic. I placed my disposable pan of Jiffy Pop on the stove's burner and gently shook it, popcorn kernels sounding like tiny firecrackers as they popped. Like many households, we had just acquired our first color TV. On it, the theme song of the western show *Bonanza* announced that it was time to settle in for the proverbial long wintry night.

The davenport opened up into a bed, and while I remember munching on popcorn and my eyelids getting heavy from studying the pawing of Little Joe's Appaloosa, I can't recall the rooftop pawing of Santa's reindeer awakening everyone in the house. The jingling of their tiny bells suddenly had my attention. I watched in awe as Santa made his way down through the attic. It occurred to me that he might change course and decide not to leave the gifts if he saw me awake. I stretched out quickly and pretended to sleep, all the while squinting to see what the gift-giver did.

He tiptoed to the Christmas tree, placed his bag of presents on the floor, and reverently bowed his head while touching Baby Jesus in the Nativity scene's manger. He made his way around the tree, studying the decorations while sampling cookies. He bent down to adjust a small toy Studebaker parked beside a cardboard house. Red crepe paper covered the house's window to reveal a glow from a little light inside. The reflection of tree lights danced in Santa's eyes as he noticed a toy deer on the floor drinking at a mirror for a pond, all positioned just so in the white cotton blanket for snow.

As he continued around the tree, he tapped the homemade ornaments in which scenes from old Christmas cards were cut with tiny nail scissors, glued onto colored tagboard, trimmed in glue and glitter, and hung on the tree. Finally, the moment came for him to reveal the gifts he brought for our family.

With great anticipation, I watched as Santa lifted a small box from his red velvet bag. He chose to leave the box open under the tree, and when he stepped back, I could scarcely contain my excitement. I had to cover my mouth to keep my gasp in check. There sat the charming Timex watch with a cream-colored leather band I'd been wanting.

Just then, I heard my name from the attic. Had Santa become stuck as he made his way back through its opening? I rubbed my eyes a few times and found it wasn't Santa calling my name.

Instead, my grandfather stood atop the ladder at the mouth of the attic. He needed my help with a package he'd been hiding up there. I worried Santa would leave with our family up and about, and sure enough, when I turned to look at the tree, he was gone.

There was no time to dwell on the disappointment of his abrupt departure. It was Christmas morning already, and there were presents to open. That was the Christmas that cemented my belief. While other children were of the opinion that Santa emerged into their homes via the chimney, I held fast to the notion that he entered my house through the attic.

Of course, there was the Christmas I feared Santa wouldn't be able to get into our house for all the decorations. My hero uncle and his fiancée planned to be married Christmas Day in our backyard. Slippery strings of beads and shells hung from our roof in preparation for the festivities. I worried Santa would not be able to get his footing and make his way in through our attic. Still, as the flower girl for the wedding, I had to stay focused on the task at hand.

Since astronaut Neil Armstrong became the first man to set foot on the moon the previous summer, an oversized book on a lectern commemorating the occasion greeted all who entered our home as the wedding guests arrived. I watched as my uncle combed the hair he'd grown to shoulder-length since he'd returned from serving our country in Vietnam. While he combed, he explained that Santa was postponing his visit to our family until after the wedding. Though I was disappointed, I knew the postponement was for the best reason I could think of—my uncle's happiness.

Once the guests were in the backyard, my uncle's soon-to-be brother-in-law played the guitar and sang. I marched down the path in my lacy white dress, tossing flower petals from my basket as I went. Bridesmaids followed, and then my soon-to-be-aunt. It was an unconventional wedding. My aunt's long-haired brother, who had received his license by mail, put down his guitar and officiated the outdoor ceremony. My aunt wore a short, cream-colored, form-fitting dress instead of the traditional long white gown. My aunt and uncle read their own wedding vows.

When the ceremony was over, I was anxious for everyone to get their quick bite of cake and gulp of punch so our family's Christmas could continue. The sooner we got to sleep, the sooner Santa would come. I was not amused that the Italian relatives my uncle just acquired seemed incapable of saying goodbye. *Andiamo* ("let's go") was tossed around like a beach ball, but no one was leaving. Thankfully, the evening mosquitoes drove the guests away. I need not have worried that our strings of beads and seashells would cause Santa to lose his footing. The next morning, we awakened to presents safe and sound under the tree.

My grandfather did not have the same good fortune as Santa that Christmas. Sporting a brand-new pair of trifocals and looking very dapper in them, he climbed a ladder to remove the wedding decorations from the roof. Suddenly, our family in the house heard a long, loud yell outside, followed by a thud. When we rushed out to see what happened, we found my grandfather rolling in the bushes. He misjudged the location of the ladder and fell from the roof to the ground. Fortunately, the only thing hurt was his pride.

We had a large date palm tree in our front yard. It was so large that passersby stopped their cars beside our brown picket fence, emerged from their vehicles with cameras, and took pictures of the giant palm. We felt like celebrities with all the attention. I always worried that Santa would have to negotiate its branches at Christmas, as if riding a bronco. The branches wildly slapped against the roof in the ocean breeze. Surely Santa must have been an adventure-seeker, though, for he always seemed to get our gifts to us and in good condition.

The one Christmas I so longed for simpler days was the one just after my fourteenth birthday. How I wished my biggest problem was figuring out Santa's method for entering our house when we had no chimney or for avoiding the hazards of our roof. That Christmas became complicated when, three weeks before Christmas Day, my grandmother who raised me had a massive heart attack and died. Her attack happened as we argued over the dishes I hadn't done.

It was a gross understatement to say I didn't feel like celebrating that Christmas. Everyone sat around opening presents, and I simply couldn't.

At their insistence, though, I managed to open one large box in the corner. Inside was a beautiful electric typewriter. My grandmother picked it out for me before she passed away. What made this gift even more special was its proof of my grandmother's love. She was harsh and cruel because of her own painful past. She believed love wasn't something said but shown. I wanted more than anything to be a writer, but I didn't realize my grandmother knew my dream or took it seriously. The typewriter demonstrated she really did love me. She just didn't know how to show it. On the hardest Christmas of all, I received the dearest gift.

As I sit here while my own grandchildren are pining for Christmas in a place where chimneys abound, I remember the quandary of my youth with no chimney for Santa's entrance. I smile at the memory of clicking keys on the electric typewriter one Christmas long ago that started my writing journey. Whether about staying in the moment with Santa's entrance through the attic or about being lost in a reverie of happier times than that of my fourteenth Christmas, what stories I have to tell my grandchildren, stories that began with Santa on the roof.

Sandy Haney devoted nearly thirty years of her life to teaching elementary school and forty years to children's ministry. Now retired, she fills her days with volunteering, speaking, and, of course, writing. She writes mostly Christian nonfiction, but she occasionally dips her toe in fiction waters. Her work appears in Servants of Grace, as well as in The Secret Place (Judson Press). Sandy has a collection of poetry, a memoir, and a mental health guide for teachers. Redemption Press has published her most recent work, *Where Are You Going?* It is a picture book to help children through the loss of a loved one. Sandy and her husband of forty-two years currently live in the Texas panhandle. They love spending time with their two grown children, their children's dream-come-true spouses, and their four delightful grandchildren.

TWELVE
THE ZOO ON THE ROOF

LAURA HARRISON

One night a loud bird
Landed on my large roof.
This is so absurd
Such an absolute goof!

The next night I awoke
A fox was barking
"I can't sleep," I spoke.
"His head, I'm marking."

Next day, I'm not kidding
A raccoon showed up.
Now, I'm not meddling
But they rode up.

A bird, fox, raccoon
All on my stupid roof
And a black balloon
Am I the one aloof?

So what did I do?
I bought a big, fat gun.
Aimed up at the blue
Shot off a few for fun.

Well, I broke a window
Made my neighbors mad
But, no one moved, you know?
Oh! I feel so bad!!!

They like it okay
No one's coming down
I'll wait 'til Sunday

And run them out of town.

Sunday came and went
The dogs scared them off
Called them magnificent
And had a good laugh.

Laura Harrison writes short stories and poems. Currently, she is working on her first novel, *Kelly's Hurdle*. She's a member of Texas High Plains Writers. She wrote the short story "Interview" in With Words We Weave: Hope. Besides writing, Laura enjoys reading mystery, romance, and literary fiction. She has a 13-year-old daughter who is an aspiring writer and artist.

THIRTEEN
WHATEVER IT TAKES

COY REECE HOLLEY

The parking lot of the church was totally empty as Barry drove in—not that unusual for a Tuesday morning, despite the controversies that had been swirling around him recently. But a piece of official-looking paper stuck out like a sore thumb on the church's front door with words Barry had been dreading for a while.

"...The Northern Federal Judicial District of Texas, Lubbock Division in the matter of Co-Plaintiffs the People of the United States of America, the People of the State of Texas, the People of the County of Hale, and the People of the City of Plainview versus Running Water Draw Cowboy Church, 5500 North Interstate 27, Plainview, Texas, and the Reverend Barry Helton both personally and in his official capacity as Senior Pastor, et al.—

"...By order of the Court of United States Magistrate Robert

Perrymore of the Lubbock Division of the Northern Federal Judicial District of Texas under emergency powers issued by the President of the United States of America, you are hereby ordered to immediately cease and desist all activities related to the practice of worship and religious instruction at the current location of the Running Water Draw Cowboy Church and are hereby ordered to appear before Magistrate Perrymore on July 7, 2035 to give reason and defense as to why this Court should not prevent you..."

That was as far and as much as Barry cared to read of that legal garbage. Barry fell on his knees and cried before God. "...Of all the stunts they could pull—now I can't even preach in front of my own congregation anymore without being arrested and put in prison. I know, Lord, what you already said about all this—but does it now have to come down to *this*?"

Despite the stellar defense team that had been defending him in federal court in Lubbock pro bono, the pressure had been on Barry since the World Health Organization and those nutjobs in Washington decided to make a big, make-believe climate-change crisis out of cow flatulence. Various commentators had been warning for years that this might happen—but did anyone ever listen?

Barry got up from in front of the church's front doors and in frustration, got back in his pickup truck to head southbound on the northbound I-27 frontage road toward the Dimmitt Highway. Barry, at the red-light intersection, first turned right into the left turn lane, then as the light began to turn yellow, turned left onto the southbound I-27 frontage road.

Barry proceeded to the on-ramp of the main highway and sped up as he merged with the rest of the traffic. He kept up his speed until he found the exit to FM 3466/Southwest Third Street. He took the exit ramp and got in the right lane. At the stop sign, Barry then turned left to go east onto Southwest Third.

As he drove, the memories flooded Barry's worried mind of his tenure on the Professional Bull Riding circuit. His days on the backs of mean ol' bulls and the injuries he suffered were some of the battle scars he still carried today. As he drove closer to the Plainview City Cemetery, he remembered the rough lifestyle of alcohol, gambling, and wild living he once led—and the terrible consequences it brought to himself, his marriage, and his kids.

That, of course, was his life before the Master rudely interrupted Barry's wild, ambitious plans. Barry's dreams of making it big at the National Finals in Vegas got cut short by a life-threatening ride that punctured his lungs, shattered several vertebrae, and broke legs that still hurt to this day.

It was in that hospital room in Vegas where the Master finally got his attention. In the middle of the night, with no one else around, an old guy who looked like his horse's vet appeared. (Was it maybe an angel? Nobody knew.) "Cowboy, if you don't change your ways, straighten up and fly right, this'll be the least of your worries. It'll be eternal destruction for you unless you get on the narrow way real soon."

The worst part for Barry in finally making his decision for Jesus Christ was in coming back home to Plainview as a prodigal son preacher's kid who was the black sheep to the man whose gravestone he headed to after getting out of the truck.

On this hot July day, Barry recalled how he came to serve the man who was known in his time as the "Apostle and Prophet to the Cowboy Nation." This man, who was both Barry's physical and spiritual father, didn't just manage to welcome him back with open arms—but also, in due time, ordained him as his successor at Running Water.

The names of his mother and daddy on the Helton Cemetery gravestone caused Barry to reflect on the months before his daddy's homegoing service. Barry's daddy had to also raise him as a single father after his mom died prematurely during his childhood due to a rare blood disease caused by a genetic condition. Daddy wasn't too happy with Barry when Barry told his dad of his desire to follow his dad's footsteps in rodeo instead of Gospel ministry.

It was sure hard for Barry and the rest of the family during the 2020 pandemic as Daddy succumbed to COVID-19 in the hospital —all alone and not allowed to even have any physical visits with his own family (much less the rest of the church).

Barry, in tears as he kneeled next to the grave, recalled his dad's last phone call to Barry when he formally transferred the leadership reins via conference call to Barry and the Running Water Church board and gave Barry his formal charge. "Barry, it's my last rodeo and my time to enter into His rest. Do whatever it takes to keep these sheep solidly focused on Him and remember what He had me teach them. Be strong and have courage; keep your eyes squarely on Him—and you will see success in everything you do."

As Barry was about to say something, an older man from out of nowhere approached him and put his arm on Barry's right shoulder. As the man did this, Barry suddenly recognized him as the same man he saw in the hospital in Vegas.

After the initial shock, Barry said to the man, "…I'm glad Daddy isn't here to see all of this. I mean—they want to finally, after all this time, take away our right to worship in the way He wants us to? Daddy didn't fight in 'Nam just for this bull crap."

The old man replied, "Barry, the Lord has a special word for you. Remember what He said about, 'To whom much is given, much shall be required.' He has much better things in store for you and your congregation. But keep in mind that it may also come with persecution. Do you also remember what Martin Niemöller said about the Holocaust?"

"No, I'm not...tell me..."

"...First, they came for the socialists, and I did not speak out because I was not a socialist. Then they came for the trade unionists, and I did not speak out because I was not a trade unionist. Then they came for the Jews, and I did not speak out—because I was not a Jew. Then they came for me—and there was no one left to speak for me."

"Barry, you now have a golden opportunity to speak volumes even in the midst of a stupid made-up climate-change emergency declared by those lousy one-worlders. But if *you* don't say something now, then who? If you don't do something now, then when? What if you're the last person in this nation still standing for freedom?"

"But if I defy this last court order, my attorneys tell me I could face federal prison time for sure!"

"Barry, who should you truly fear—the God who you say you serve or this modern-day government version of Caesar? Is not He who is greater in you better than he who is in the world?"

Back at the barn behind his house, Barry rearranged his tack and helped settle down his horse for the night. The words that the old man said to him at Daddy's grave really threw him for a loop. After all, the press attention brought upon him and Running

Water from the federal court case had really worn him down. And the news he'd gotten from his attorneys hadn't been all that great lately, either. It seemed like he'd truly used all his aces, indeed.

Until, that was, when he looked upon his horse… Did Barry really want to risk all of the time and expense he'd put into training ol' Tomato? *He's my best workhorse…always dependable, obedient, and faithful when I need him most.* If there was truly a time when Barry's back was against the wall, it was now.

"Okay, Lord—I know it's against my better judgment…but I don't know what else to do now… Whatever it takes…" Barry then put his right arm behind Tomato's neck and whispered, "Tomato, ol' boy—I really hate to ask you to do what I'm about to ask you to do. But our backs are against the wall—and I really need your help on this one. Pardner—can I really trust you to help me with this?"

With a trusting look in his eyes, Tomato seemed to respond back to his master with, "…Whatever you need me to do, Boss. Just lead me where you want me to go, and I'll follow you like I always have."

Barry softly said to his mount, "Thanks, ol' boy… I knew I could count on you." Barry then pulled out his cell phone and started texting several people about his upcoming plans.

Several days later

"Breaking news for you on this Sunday morning… In defiance of a court order by Federal Magistrate Robert Perrymore and Presidential climate-change orders, a Texas cowboy preacher and pastor has staged a very unique form of protest. Alana Alexander reports live from his church in Plainview, Texas. Alana?"

"Chuck, the cars are lined up jam-packed for several miles up and down I-27 as Barry Helton, pastor of the Running Water Draw Cowboy Church, has turned his regular Sunday morning church service into a protest that he calls a 'Sermon on the Mount on the Roof.' Pastor Helton, after receiving notice of a restraining order against him by Magistrate Perrymore, believe it or not, is planning to preach a sermon outdoors on top of his church roof while mounted on his horse, Tomato. The cars are lined up and down the length of I-27 inside the Plainview city limits, listening to this drive-up church service being broadcast on local radio, similar to that seen during the 2020 COVID pandemic.

"...Plainview police, as well as county, state, and federal law enforcement, are surrounding the church building and trying to keep protestors away from the church building while also trying to talk Pastor Helton into coming down off the roof and submitting to authorities. As the special music portion of the service concludes, let's now cut to the roof as Pastor Helton begins his remarks..."

"...To the members of Running Water as well as the rest of the world, I declare to you that this day, from here on out, will be known as a pivotal day in the history of our nation. This despicable climate-change emergency order that has come down from the President himself and his one-worlder establishment cronies is an absolute slap in the face to the memory of my own father, who honorably served his country in the jungles of Vietnam. I fear our country has now sold its sovereignty and soul for a mess of one-world government slop and porridge! And we, as believers in Jesus/Y'shua, will no longer stand for these unjust rules and regulations that will lock us down just like we were back in 2020. And if I have to preach this sermon on my horse against it to draw attention, so be it!"

"Chuck, this is a developing situation. We'll keep you posted…"

"Alana, before you go away, I've got to know—how in the world did Pastor Helton get his horse on that church roof?"

"Chuck, sources tell us that it was no easy task for Pastor Helton to do so—especially on very short notice. And quite expensive and labor intensive for a church of their size to do, as far as specific logistics were concerned. But according to a statement given by the church, officials also tell us that Pastor Helton felt so strongly against the recent controversial emergency orders that he saw no other option to make his case known than to take this extremely drastic action."

"Thanks, Alana. If there are any further developments on this story, we'll keep you advised. We now return you back to your regular programming."

Coy Reece Holley is a graduate of both South Plains College and Eastern New Mexico University. Mr. Holley has previously written for the Lubbock Avalanche-Journal and the New Mexico MICLine and also served as the Contributing Editor for Texas Culture and Politics and Managing Editor for Asia, Africa, South America, and Other Regions for the now defunct Suite101.com. Mr. Holley has also served as a production and news assistant for Rhattigan Broadcasting (now High Plains Radio Network). He currently serves as a freelance journalist and writes a weekly faith column called "Coy RH At The CROSSRoads" for the Hearst Community Media Group. He has also written and self-published several evangelical Christian-based books that are currently available via Amazon and also through his online publishing company, Broken and Shattered Promises Online Publishing and

Productions. For more detailed information on any of Coy's current releases, please go to https://coyrhseatcbspm.wixsite.com/walking.

FOURTEEN
FOR A FAVOR

LYNETTE JALUFKA

Sir Guy stepped out of the tent and was met with a strong wind. Not a good day for a joust. He folded his arms in an attempt to keep himself on the ground. He would have to hold the lance very still in the day's tournament. All around him, colorful pavilions rustled, even making the horses unsettled.

Suddenly, a whirlwind twisted past him. Something thin and yellow flew in it. A snake? Nay, it was something else. Guy was intrigued. He followed the whirlwind until it crawled up the side of a large green and black pavilion and disappeared, depositing the yellow item on a center pole just below the same-colored banner containing a charging boar.

Guy had seen that animal before. It belonged to Sir Baldric, the knight who unhorsed him at the last tournament and took his horse Thunder as a prize. Since then, Guy's confidence had waned. With his meager supply of money, he was forced to get an old nag that he wasn't sure could make it through one round. He needed to win.

He gazed at the fluttering yellow object on the pole. Now he knew what it was: a ribbon. More importantly, a lady's favor. His blood grew hot. How careless of a knight to lose a lady's favor, the object that signified he was her champion in the tournament. How Guy wished he could carry one while he charged at his opponent, knowing that a lady chose him. Him! He would fight for her. But alas, no lady ever chose him. And who would choose him now?

But then, what if the lady lost the ribbon? Would she have another to give her champion? The ribbon glittered in the sunlight. It obviously had gold thread in it. Someone had taken great care to make it.

That did it. Guy would rescue that ribbon and try to return it to the owner, if she could be found. All before the tournament started. And without disturbing Sir Baldric and his retinue inside.

This was not going to be easy. He could not climb onto the roof of the tent like he could if it were a building. And he would have to reach the center of it.

A horse nickered, causing him to turn. It was Thunder! He went to the horse and untied the animal. "Good lad. Keep quiet." He led the horse around to the back of the tent. Then he vaulted onto the stallion's bare back. Thunder did not move. Guy slowly stood on his back, the wind making it hard to balance. Then he drew his sword and stretched it toward the center pole. It did not reach. He tried standing on his toes. Just a little bit farther.

His feet began to slide down Thunder's side. Suddenly, he fell forward, grasping the canvas roof with his hands. Shouts were heard from inside.

Guy pulled himself up onto the supporting poles.

Crack!

The supporting poles inside would not hold him. He scrambled to the center.

Now Sir Baldric's booming voice sounded through the fabric. "What the devil is happening, you fools?"

Guy grabbed the ribbon as the poles gave way and crashed to the ground. He quickly rose and ran through the fabric and down a pathway before he could be spotted.

He should slow down. Otherwise, people might think he had done something bad. He looked back to see if he was being pursued. "Oof!"

Someone had blocked his progress. He fell to the ground in a tangle of cloth. When he stopped and righted himself, he realized he had collided with a woman. Not just any woman. A lady, by the fine way she was dressed.

He reached out a hand and helped her to her feet. "Pardon me, my lady. I was not looking where I was going."

She kept looking at the ground. "Nor was I."

"The fault is mine. Are you hurt?"

"Nay," she said with a sob. She still would not look at him.

Was she crying? She must be in pain. "Lady, I will fetch help. You're hurting."

She put a hand on his arm and looked straight at him with red eyes and a dirty, tear-stained face. "Nay! What is hurting me you cannot help."

Guy was taken aback. "Did someone hurt you?"

Tears flowed down her dirty cheek. "If I tell you, will you go away?"

What an odd request. She should not be left alone. "Upon my word, I will."

She gave him a strange look. "You will think me silly, like my sisters."

"Nay. Pray tell, what is it?"

She looked back at the ground. "This is my first time at a tournament. So I took a yellow ribbon and embroidered it with gold thread. I wanted to give it to a knight in the tournament today. But my sisters are prettier than I. And they chose the ones I wanted. The other knights won't look at me. And then this terrible wind took my favor away."

Guy glanced at the ribbon held tightly in his hand. The gold thread sparkled in the sunlight. It could be no other. "Lady, here. Is this your favor?" He stretched out his hand.

Her eyes opened wide. "Oh, thank you, thank you, good sir! It is. It is! God answered my prayer." She snatched it from his hand. "How did you find it?"

"God must have helped, for the wind brought it to me." He did not think she needed to know about his destroying Sir Baldric's tent. "And now, dear lady, may I have the honor of being your champion and wearing your favor in the tournament?"

"You are in the tournament?"

He bowed. "Sir Guy, at your service. And what may I call you?"

"Lady Amelia." She smiled so that her eyes were nearly covered by her cheeks. "I would be glad to have such a kindhearted knight who rescues lost favors for my champion." She tied the favor on his arm.

By the end of the day, Sir Baldric learned what it felt like to be unhorsed, and Thunder returned to Guy's camp.

FIFTEEN
A GRAY DAY STORY

ASHLYN PARKER

Some nights, I lie with my three-year-old to help him go to sleep. We turn toward each other on our pillows, our faces silhouetted in the light of the nightlight, and he asks me to tell him a "Gray Day Story"—a make-believe story about him as a prince in a blue castle surrounded by water infested with sharks and spinosauruses. Or a story with him and his chocolate lab running into snapping turtles and Bigfoot (who is actually a good guy, he insists).

It's in these little moments I'm challenged most as a storyteller, thinking of a conflict and resolution on the spot. But I can see his eyes twinkle in the dark with each tale. His little mind is a sponge, and before long, he knows how to make up his own bedtime stories and tell them to me.

In this instance, as we lie wrapped up in covers, I ask him: "Tell me about what was on the roof that one day." His eyebrows shoot up as he goes into a long ramble of characters, scenes, and conflicts I hurry to write down. I have added *many* details to help push the story along, but all of the following storylines come straight from his world of creativity:

A rooster woke up bright and early one morning. He was starving, and that was the only thing on his mind. He needed a worm, bad. But today, he didn't plan on digging through the dirt, searching with all the other chickens. He didn't want just a little worm—he wanted the biggest worm of all.

So the rooster flapped his wings, and he went up, up, up into the sky. He landed on top of the barn roof with a thud and ruffled his feathers. No other chicken had checked up here for worms ever before. He knew there was one hiding just for him.

He strutted through some twigs and branches but found no worms. He almost slipped down the steep side once, but he kept on. His tummy was still rumbling for a slimy breakfast.

Then the rooster heard something rustling in a pile of leaves near the end of the roof. He was scared to go over there. Whatever it was, it was *big*. Curious, he walked over and bobbed his head closer to take a peek.

Before he could move the leaves, a huge pink snake lunged at him!

He BAAAWWWKED and flapped his wings as hard as he could away from the beast. He fell backward and started to roll. He dug his claws into the tin with a screech and tried to balance himself with his wings until he finally slowed to a stop. He knew the snake was coming for him now. All he wanted was breakfast, but now he was going to be the snack!

But the snake didn't come toward him. The rooster peeked toward the leaves and saw it wiggling around, minding its own business. That was when the rooster noticed it was ooey and gooey and it wasn't a snake at all. It was the worm of his dreams!

The rooster ran as fast as he could toward the worm, and when he reached it, he slurped it up like a big spaghetti noodle. It was delicious! He was almost done when he felt wiggling and squiggling all over his tummy. It felt like his tummy was getting tickled from the inside!

The rooster spit out the worm as fast as he could and said, "SHOOSHEY!" Once he hit the ground, the worm dragged itself back to the leaves and started to sob.

The rooster didn't know worms could cry. He felt really bad.

The rooster went to the worm and told him he was sorry. The worm forgave him but said he just wanted his mom. The rooster asked the worm where she was, but he didn't know. He missed his mom and wanted her to come home.

The rooster was still hungry, but he felt like the baby worm needed his help. So he tucked the worm into his bed of leaves and told him he would go find mama worm.

The rooster glided from the roof and landed onto a tree branch. He used his bird's-eye view to try and spot the worm on the ground. He was looking all over when he heard something move next to him, something in the trunk of the tree.

The rooster moved closer to the sound of rustling and found it was coming from a hole. He was scared, but he found the courage to peek his beak inside.

He couldn't believe his eyes! The biggest worm he had ever seen was curled up, sleeping right next to a squirrel. But the squirrel was far from resting. She was hurriedly gathering pinecones onto her lap.

The squirrel jumped up and pushed past the rooster on her way out of her home. She went out onto the branch with her pinecones and began throwing them as hard as she could into the pond below. They were making a huge splash each time she did, and if she ran out, the squirrel returned to her hole to get more.

All of a sudden, an owl in the next tree over stuck his head from the leaves and shouted, "WHO, WHO IS MAKING THAT NOISE?"

The squirrel hurled another pinecone into the water and told the owl she had a very, very important job to do. The owl said, "NO, NO! I CAN'T SLEEP!"

The squirrel stopped and told the owl, "Well, everyone else is sleeping! There's a giant worm in my bed, snoozing, and all the other animals aren't awake. But the sun is already up! I have to help wake everyone up to start the day!"

That was when the rooster realized something. He was supposed to crow this morning. His cock-a-doodle-doo was what woke the entire farm up for the day, but he forgot to do it because he was so hungry!

He huffed and puffed up as big as he could and sounded the alarm extra loud with a COCK-A-DOODLE-DOO! He did it three more times and began to hear the chickens rustling, cows mooing, and the dogs yawning.

Then the mama worm stopped snoring and poked her head out of the hole. The rooster told her about the baby worm crying for her. He asked the worm if she trusted him, and she thought for a long time. She did *not* trust the rooster, but she needed her baby. She finally nodded her head yes.

The rooster bent down, and the worm slid her way onto his back and wrapped around him tight. He flapped his wings as hard as he could, and they flew to the roof. After they landed, the mama worm wiggled free from his back and went to the leaves. Her baby squealed with delight! They curled together into a ball, but the rooster knew it really was a big hug.

The rooster smiled. It felt good that he helped the mama worm and her baby get back together. He was glad he finally remembered to do his most important job—starting the day—because the early bird doesn't always get the worm. Sometimes, the early bird wakes up the farmer, who puts on his boots and clothes and sprinkles out chicken scratch for him to gobble up like a turkey.

And today, that would taste just fine. In fact, he had a feeling that might just be his new favorite food.

*Here's how the story actually went:

A rooster was trying to find some worms.

He saw a snake…wait, it wasn't a snake. It was a worm! It was as big as a snake. It was on the roof.

The worm was looking for its mom, and he ate the worm. He spit the worm out because it was shooshey!

He needed to go find its mom. He looked in a tree, and his mom was sleeping with a soft animal, a squirrel, and the squirrel was everywhere!

The squirrel had pinecones, and he was throwing them in water. A mama owl said to the squirrel, "No, no squirrel!"

She was waking up the rooster's sunshine. She was trying to wake the people up.

The rooster said, "Good job! It's time to start the day and get clothes and shoes on!"

I will cling to these times of how simple it is to make each other smile. While most Gray Day stories fade away shortly after they're told, I'm proud this one will bring us a little ray of happiness in years to come.

Ashlyn Parker is a small-town author and boy mom who specializes in journalism and children's stories. You can follow her latest projects on @AshlynTheWriter on Twitter.

SIXTEEN
UNROOFING THE ROOF

JAMES D. QUIGGLE

About AD 30, there was a man unable to voluntarily move his limbs. His friends carried him about on a bed. Now, this bed was little more than a padded quilt, at most a thin mattress. Four friends were needed, and this man had four friends who loved him. They carried him wherever he needed to go.

Then one day, the four friends heard a miracle-worker was in town. They decided to take their friend to the healer. But they could not get their friend close enough to the healer for the healer to heal their friend.

"What to do?" they asked. If they could just get him to this healer, they were sure their friend would be healed. But the crowds were so great that even the way to the door was covered by dozens and dozens of people. There was just no way.

Then one of them thought, "The roof!" The roof on the house

was flat. In those days, people used the roof for storage or a quiet place for prayer. People would eat and sleep on the roof when the weather was hot. Most roofs were made of tiles of mud and clay. But sometimes, on some roofs, people grew grass, making a roof a nice place to visit and rest.

There was a stair at the side of the house leading to the flat, mud-tiled roof. The four friends struggled to get their friend up on the roof. They tied four ropes to the four corners of the bed. Then, little by little, by lifting and pulling, the friends brought their friend to the flat roof on the house where the healer was healing the people.

They had a plan. They would dig through the roof, removing the mud tiles to unroof the roof, right over the place where the healer was healing. They dug through the roof; they let down the bed into the house using the ropes they had lifted the bed up onto the house. The ceiling was not too high, so the distance was not too great.

Let us imagine the scene. The healer is at the door of the house, or perhaps just outside the door. The custom of the times was to sit to teach, so he might have been sitting on a chair in the doorway. The people inside the house—the wives, children, and servants—heard the four men breaking into the house through the roof. Perhaps they thought, *Our house isn't safe from these crowds!* Or perhaps, *Our home and family are not safe when the healer is in the house.* Perhaps they simply wondered, *Why is someone breaking into the house?*

The bed with the man was lowered through the roof to the floor. Two of the men jumped down into the house; then the other two. "We've brought our friend to be healed." The people in the house hurried to get the healer's attention. But the healer had seen what happened. And "seeing their faith," the healer said to the man on the bed, "Son, your sins are forgiven."

Only this one man, in the midst of crowds struggling to catch the healer's attention, out of all the people he had already healed and all those waiting to be healed, did the healer call "son."

It is an amazing moment of tenderness, of compassion; and it is revealing. Those who would serve others must serve with compassion for those to whom they minister. A paralyzed man was considered a burden to his family. He was unable to make any contribution to the welfare of others. It is amazing that the four men thought to bring the man to this healer, this Jesus of Nazareth. But by their faith, they did, and their friend was healed.

Now, there were some in the crowd who were offended. They were the religious, the theologians of the day. "Why," they said within themselves and quietly to one another, "does this one in this manner speak blasphemies? Who is able to forgive sins if not one, God?"

Jesus might have said, "Be healed," or "May your sins be forgiven." But he had said, "Your sins are forgiven," because he really did have the authority and power to forgive sins. But he also said what he said as a deliberate provocation to provide an opportunity to reveal some things about himself. Jesus had healed the man's conscience before healing his body and thereby greatly strengthened his faith.

Now, when the theologians heard Jesus claim to forgive sins, their heresy alarms sounded. Only God has the authority to forgive sin. They drew the immediately available conclusion: Jesus was speaking blasphemy by claiming to have the authority to forgive sin. Blasphemy is any evil-speaking against a person, and in this instance, evil-speaking concerning God. The ability to forgive sins belonged to God alone. For a human being to claim to have that ability was to claim to be God, thereby lowering God to the level of human beings. That was the blasphemy.

Jesus knew the thoughts of the theologians. His response was to ask a question. "Is it easier to say, 'Your sins are forgiven,' or to say, 'Get up, pick up your bed, and walk?'" Now, it is much easier to say, "Your sins are forgiven," than to say, "Get up, pick up your bed, and walk." No one can see if sins are truly forgiven, but everyone can see if a paralyzed man can get up and walk. No one has to prove he is able to forgive sins, he just has to say it. But to tell a paralyzed man to get up and walk, well, the proof is in the getting up and walking!

That was why Jesus asked the question to the theologians—to prove he had the power to forgive sins, by proving he could heal the man.

Healing the disease convincingly demonstrated the authority to forgive sin. Jesus did not state he had been given authority to forgive sins, but that he possessed that authority; the authority to forgive sin was innate to his essential being. Jesus is not denying his humanity, nor is he denying the theologians' premise that only God can forgive sin. Jesus is deliberately revealing his humanity is vested with divine authority and ability, and he is giving the theologians and the crowd the opportunity to recognize he is God come to Earth to forgive sin.

The formerly paralyzed man's reaction was faith. Undoubtedly, he felt a change in his body, perhaps sensation in limbs formerly devoid of feeling. But there is always a moment when faith must be put to the test. His test was to get out of bed and walk. The test was not only faith his body had been healed, but faith his sins had been forgiven. Notice there is no process to Jesus's healing work. In all but one case (Mark 8:24–25), Jesus healed instantly.

The crowd's reaction, which was to the healing, not the forgiveness (most might not have heard the conversation), was to glorify God; but not God in the Person of Jesus the God-man. Healing the man let down through the roof was one of the first steps in many steps to reveal himself as the one with the authority and power to forgive sin.

SEVENTEEN
FARM GIRL

BETTY M. REEVES

I liked being a farmer's daughter, and I loved living on the farm.

Our farm was four-and-a-half miles away from town. That was three miles of two-lane highway and a mile and a half of dirt road. Two cars or pickups could meet and pass by each other if they slowed down and scrunched close to the edges of the dirt road.

I liked the bar ditch on the far side of the dirt road, where the neighbor had big sunflowers growing. The flower heads always faced the sun.

I could not play in that bar ditch because the leaves of the big sunflowers made me itch and sneeze. When I broke off any of the baby flowers, gooey stuff got on me. I would pull off flower petals and say, "Eeny Meeney Miney Moe," or "He loves me, he loves me not," and all that. Momma didn't like those flowers, so I didn't take any into the house.

On the far side of the sunflowers was the neighbor's fenced cow pasture. I was not allowed to go there because the neighbor had a bull who did not like kids. At least, that was what my momma and daddy told me. They also told me that when I was a toddler, I once wandered into that pasture. I was lucky, they said, that I didn't get hurt.

The bar ditch on our side of the dirt road was just red clay dirt because Daddy kept it graded with a blade he put on his green John Deere tractor. I could play there. But it was dirty, and when I went to the house, I was covered in sticky red dirt. Momma would shake her head, but she smiled anyway.

Other nice things about being a farm girl were:

1. On clear nights, I could see the stars across the whole sky and all the way to the ground. Sometimes, I saw shooting stars. At Christmas, I tried to spot Santa Claus and his reindeer.

2. I could run around barefoot. I knew the places to avoid where goat heads or grass burrs might be. If I was wrong, Momma would help me get rid of the sticker in my foot.

3. I could play with horny toads and their teeny, tiny babies. Boy, those critters were fast! Momma said they were really horned lizards, but when I said that to a boy in Sunday school, he called me an egghead.

4. I could hunt tadpoles in the playa lake on the north forty acres. Our playa lake would only show when we had plenty of rain or when irrigation water ran into it. Daddy said the playa lake was good for the Ogallala Aquifer under the ground where we got our well water.

5. Best of all was on Sundays after church, when my brother and I could have friends come home with us for the whole day!

We belonged to the First Methodist Church, but there wasn't a Second Methodist Church in town. The population of the town was about 900 people, with a Baptist Church, a Church of Christ, and our Methodist Church, all on the same gravel road. If there were other churches in town, they were not on the same road and I didn't know about them.

When we had a friend over, they were with us on the farm after Sunday school and church service, through dinner, all afternoon, for supper, and until evening church service. That was when we took them back to their folks at church. The next Sunday or sometime after that, we could swap and go home with one of our friends.

One Sunday afternoon, I saw my brother and his friend jump off the roof of our well house. The older boys did not appreciate my tagging along, so they dared me to jump off the roof, too.

I thought, *If they can do it, so can I.* While I was thinking about it, the boys took off. I didn't even notice they were gone.

The small red well house was probably five feet square. It was only large enough for two metal boxes, a bunch of pipes curlicued around like what was under the sink in our bathroom, plus what looked like a water heater. It was hot in the well house, and I was not supposed to be inside it.

But nobody told me I could not be on top of it.

The roof of the well house sloped one way only. I think the short side was at least a foot taller than Daddy, or maybe seven feet off the ground. It did not have shingles like the house had. Instead, the roof was covered with one big black tar sheet with tiny green gravel all over it. I knew I would have to be careful, because that gravel could be pretty rough on hands and legs.

Behind the well house was some of Daddy's farm equipment that I liked to climb on, over, under, and around. I could pretend to be a trapeze artist or a tightrope walker. I figured my brother and his friend climbed the farm equipment to get on the roof. So that was what I did, too.

It didn't take long to figure out how to balance on the slanted roof.

I remember jumping. It felt great, but I landed on my hands and knees! So I decided to do it better the next time.

I was in midair when Momma looked out the kitchen window and saw me.

She raced out the door and sailed over the back steps.

I landed squarely on my feet and ran to meet her.

I thought it was a great jump! Momma did not.

I was laughing! Momma was not.

She made me promise to never do that again. I never did, but I had lots of other fun adventures. Momma wasn't too keen on some of them, either.

By the time this anthology is published, Betty M. Reeves will have completed a Christian historical fiction series for kids from five years old to teens and young adults. Two books in The Story of Glops series were nominated for Christian Indie Awards. Betty has also written two music books. She has not decided what to write next. Betty and her husband, Glenn, live in Borger and Amarillo. They have a large, growing family and a cute Yorkie.

EIGHTEEN
LOOK AT THAT VIEW

CINDY RIOS

Lonnie nailed the last board on the railing around his new deck on the roof and reached into the cooler for a bottle of water. After pouring it over his sweat-soaked head, he pulled off his work gloves and ran his hand over the smooth, pressure-treated wood. He could hear Rabbit Creek running fast behind the house and wondered if the fish were biting. All the rain lately had put him way behind schedule, and he was aching to go down and throw a line in the water.

He climbed down the staircase and hollered, "Nita Dawn, come check this out. You're gonna love it."

The screen door slammed, and his wife came stomping down the porch steps, hands on her hips and a dish towel thrown over her left shoulder. "I'll tell you what I'd love. To be on a cruise ship holding a cold drink with one of those tiny umbrellas in it." She grabbed the towel and started swatting Lonnie on the head.

"That's what I'd love. But no. You had to go and use the money in our vacation fund for a pile of lumber and a box of nails."

Lonnie reached out to pat her arm, but she slapped his hand away. He'd expected this reaction and was determined to stay positive. "Now, honey, just think. We can sit up there and have a few beers, and I can cook us some steaks. Come on and see what you think." He hurried up the stairs ahead of her and opened the big umbrella to shade the table he'd built from the extra wood. As soon as he figured out how to get the barbecue grill up there, it would be perfect.

Nita Dawn took her time coming up the stairs, and when she got to the top, she walked over to the edge, past two old aluminum lawn chairs, each covered with a faded towel. She looked out past the yard to the creek. "The water's higher than I've ever seen it. If we get any more rain, it'll be up in the yard. I'm worried about my chickens, Lonnie."

The brightly painted turquoise coop sat halfway between the house and the creek. The chickens were free to roam all day, until Nita Dawn called them by name every evening to get in the coop for the night. They rewarded her with more eggs than she and Lonnie could eat, and the extras were sold at a roadside stand, giving her a tidy little sum every week.

"Those chickens will be okay, honey. The last time that creek flooded was back in '76 when Grandaddy and Mee-maw still lived here. Took out the barn and the goat pen. They didn't have chickens, though." Lonnie shook his head, remembering the summers spent out here when he was a kid. "Look at that view. Mee-maw would've loved this deck. And I made the railing nice and sturdy so that when we have kids, it'll be safe for them to come up here, too."

Nita Dawn grabbed the towels and started back down the

stairs, almost knocking over the TV tray holding a citronella candle and two coasters from their honeymoon in Branson. "You need to replace those chairs, Lonnie. That frayed webbing is tacky. And I told you, we're not having a baby until I'm at least twenty-five." The screen door slammed behind her, and thunder rumbled in the distance. The earthy smell of coming rain hung heavy in the air.

For the next two weeks, it rained almost nonstop. The creek overflowed its banks, coming dangerously close to the chicken coop. Lonnie spent hours sitting under the big umbrella, watching the rising water, trying to figure out some way to make Nita Dawn happy. She hadn't spoken to him in days, and he was beginning to question spending their vacation money building a deck on the roof. He knew if he could just get her to stay up there with him for a couple of hours, have some beers and a nice dinner, she would start to love it as much as he did. After a quick trip to the store, he would put that plan in motion.

"Honey, I'm going to run into town. You need anything?" Lonnie grabbed his keys and his favorite Bass Pro camo cap. "I'm going to Walmart." When she didn't answer, he got in his pickup and left. The road to town was away from the still-rising creek, so he shouldn't have any problem getting there and back.

Lonnie had plenty of time on the twenty-five-mile drive into town to think about how unhappy Nita Dawn was these days. He had promised her on their wedding day that he would do everything he could to make her dreams come true. When Meemaw passed away and Lonnie inherited the house and land, Nita Dawn was so excited to leave their tiny apartment in town and move out to the country. But as soon as she realized the mansion she was hoping for was really a run-down farmhouse, her enthusiasm dimmed.

When he pulled the pickup back into the hard-packed dirt driveway, Lonnie saw his wife sitting on the porch with a chicken under one arm and another in her lap. She was smoking a cigarette, and that was not a good sign.

"Hey, honey. I got a couple of steaks and a box of real nice strawberries. Maybe you can make us some shortcake." Lonnie carried the bags of groceries into the kitchen and plopped them on the worn counter.

Nita Dawn came into the house and set the chickens down on the floor. "I don't feel like making shortcake, Lonnie. You shoulda just got those little sponge cake thingies. And I bet you probably forgot the whipped cream, too." She unloaded the bags and started to put away the items. When she came to the steaks, she turned around, holding the package. "Top sirloin? Really, Lonnie? You know I like a T-bone or even a New York strip, and you bring home top sirloin." She opened the refrigerator and tossed the meat onto the nearly empty shelf.

"I'm sorry, baby. Sirloin was the cheapest. You know they've cut my hours at work. That's why I had so much free time to spend on building the deck." He pulled off his cap and ran his fingers through his curly blond hair. "You've been so sad lately, and I just wanted to do something to cheer you up. Me and Harv got the grill up there yesterday while you were getting your nails done." It had taken some careful maneuvering, but the big Traeger Pro-Series thirty-four-inch pellet grill now resided on the new deck, safe from the rising waters of Rabbit Creek.

Three hours later, Lonnie carried the leftovers from dinner down the outside staircase and into the kitchen. Nita Dawn hadn't even bothered to come up to the deck to eat the perfectly cooked steak, and she sure hadn't made any shortcake. After cleaning the dishes, he grabbed another beer from the fridge and walked into the living room, where his wife was scrolling through pictures on her phone.

"Whatcha doing, honey?" Lonnie sat down on the lumpy couch beside her and saw she was on a travel website looking at pictures of tropical beaches filled with tanned, smiling people splashing in the turquoise water. "Can you imagine getting sand all up in your swimsuit and sticking to your sunscreen?" he asked. "That's not what I call a vacation. You can get all the sun you want up on our deck for free."

Nita Dawn slowly put her phone on the coffee table, turned to him, and said, "Lonnie Tucker, you are about the most clueless husband I have ever seen. When are you gonna get it through your thick head that I do not want anything to do with that stupid deck up on the roof? I will never set foot up there again, so you might as well forget it." She grabbed her phone and stomped through the kitchen and out the back door, calling the chickens to the coop for the night.

It was after midnight when Lonnie woke up to Nita Dawn shaking his arm. "Lonnie, the floor is wet. Why is there water on the floor?" She was standing by the side of the bed, looking down. "We must have a busted pipe or something."

Lonnie jumped out of bed and splashed through the ankle-deep water to the kitchen. He knew before he looked out the window what was happening. The creek had risen enough to flood the house. He grabbed a flashlight and took a deep breath before opening the back door to a cold and muddy rushing wave that covered the kitchen floor. "Come on, Nita Dawn. We gotta get out of here." He ran back to the bedroom and grabbed his wife's arm. "We'll be safer up on the roof."

They made their way out of the house and started up the

staircase. The water was getting deeper by the minute, and he saw a big clump of white feathers in the beam of the flashlight.

"Lonnie, wait. My chickens." Nita Dawn held on to the stair rail and reached out, but the water was moving too fast. "No. Bernadette, come back." She stood halfway up the stairs and started screaming the names of the birds as they floated by. "Lucy, Penny, Bonnie. Not my sweet girls." She sobbed, her tears mixing with the pouring rain as Lonnie led her up the stairs. She sat at the table under the umbrella, which was useless since she was already soaking wet. Looking down at her bare feet, she said, "I don't have any shoes on. I need my flip-flops." She twisted the thin, gold wedding band round and round her finger.

At the back of the deck, the side that faced the creek, Lonnie stood at the railing and watched as the rushing water carried branches, a lawn chair, and various other objects past the beam of his flashlight. He never heard Nita Dawn's footsteps behind him, but he felt the shove, and before he could grab hold of anything, he was over the edge. The cold, muddy waters of Rabbit Creek carried him off into the dark night.

Six weeks later, Nita Dawn sat on the balcony of her suite on the Caribbean Princess, watched the rising sun reflect off the ocean, and smiled. "Look at that view."

She finished her coffee and went inside to dress. The little black bikini and some flip-flops bedazzled with rhinestones would be perfect for her first morning by the pool. Tucking her hair up under a wide-brimmed straw hat, she adjusted the little black veil that hung almost to her chin. She was in mourning, after all.

The elevator doors opened to the Lido deck, where tropical music played and bartenders poured drinks with little umbrellas into tall glasses shaped like pineapples. Nita Dawn claimed a deck lounger on the second level and spread her towel. It wasn't long before she saw other passengers fill the area, smearing SPF 50 on their noisy children and shouting for them to "stay where I can see you" before gulping the first of many rum punches and other colorful adult beverages.

Nita Dawn ordered one such drink from a roaming waiter and was digging in her bag for her own sunscreen when a voice spoke from the lounger on her left.

"Is this your first cruise?" the woman asked.

"Yes, it is. You?"

"No, our fifth. It's the first time we've brought the kids, though." The woman scanned the pool and then turned back to Nita Dawn. "I've never seen a sun hat with a veil before. That's cute."

Nita Dawn gave the woman the smile she had been practicing. The one that she called her sad smile. "Oh, thank you. It didn't come that way. I added it because I'm in mourning, and in the South, where I come from, veils and wearing black are expected for the first thirty days for sure, but preferably for six months." She stopped and then added, "I'm from Alabama. My name's Nita Dawn Tucker, and my husband, Lonnie, was tragically killed just six weeks ago." She sniffed and dabbed at her eyes with her pinkie, careful not to mess up the eyeliner she'd applied earlier.

"I'm so sorry." The woman patted Nita Dawn's shoulder. "I'm Margie Delaney. We're from Texas. My husband's still in bed with a major hangover." Turning toward the pool, she shouted, "Lucas Delaney, quit holdin' your sister's head under the water. Don't make me get up and come over there."

"How old are your children?" Nita Dawn asked as she watched Margie suck down the remainder of what appeared to be a frozen piña colada and wave to the waiter for another. She'd be drinking like that, too, if those kids were hers.

"Lucas turns twelve tomorrow, and Hollis Anne turns ten on Friday. We told them this trip was their birthday present. But I can tell you right now, we shoulda thought twice about that." Margie closed her eyes and lay back. "Do you have kids?"

"No. Lonnie and I had only been married just a little over three years when he passed. He wanted to wait…" Nita Dawn fanned herself, and the two-carat diamond ring on her left hand sparkled in the tropical sun. "I can't believe he's really gone." Thank God she had used the egg money to buy that big insurance policy. A girl had to be prepared.

Margie turned toward Nita Dawn and said in a quiet voice, "I'm a good listener, if you wanna talk about it."

"Well, you see, he drowned when the creek behind the house flooded. He was washed away. It was at night…and the water had risen really fast. It was already ankle-deep when we woke up. I lost my husband and all my chickens." Nita Dawn sniffed and closed her eyes as she lay back on the lounger.

"Well, holy crap, girl," Margie said in a stunned voice. "Sounds like you're lucky to be here today."

Nita Dawn smiled that sad smile and said, "Yes, I surely am. You see, my sweet Lonnie had just finished building a deck on the roof, and he made sure I was safely up there. But when I turned around, he was gone. Swept away, just like my chickens." She wiped away a tear. "My poor, sweet chickens. I sure do miss them."

· · ·

Cindy Rios is a writer of cozy mysteries, short stories, and flash fiction. She is a lifelong resident of the Texas panhandle and gets inspiration from the stark beauty of flat vistas and the majesty of Palo Duro Canyon. When she's not thinking up ways to murder her characters, she likes to spend time with her children and grandchildren and travel with her artist husband.

NINETEEN
THE ROOF OF THE WORLD

KARL SMITH

The greatest adventures of my life were in the woods and rivers of Missouri. How could a child not have a memorable youth growing up wild and free in the backwoods of such a place? I camped and hiked alone most of the time and relied on a pocketknife as my main, and usually only, tool. I listened well to the old-timers and the native men and women as they told stories of long-forgotten times. I find it a duty and joy to pass on the skills I learned from the old-timers to new generations—that is, now that I find myself an old-timer. I return now and again to those lessons and adventures and smile with my heart that God did bless me with abundant joy in humble pursuits. Listen now to a tale.

Here I am on adventure to the Salt River in the fall. It is a much younger me as I walk out the back door and follow the shortcut to grade school, but when I reach the creek branch, I turn off the path, follow the branch downstream to Lick Creek, and continue on 'til I reach the South Fork of the Salt. I am confident as I walk on the rocks and sand in the creek bed until the water becomes deeper. I then find the trail that will take me farther down the bank of Lick Creek. As I walk along, I wonder how many feet have worn this trail so deeply into the bank. How many centuries have young boys sought adventure along this path? Now I seek supper and a comfortable place to camp. I arrive on the banks of the Salt late in the afternoon.

I carry my kit: some matches dipped in paraffin with a goodly length of string wrapped around them, a pocketknife, a small tarpaulin, and a fishhook. I also carry an apple for a snack and a pack of gum. I plan to catch my supper from the Salt and spend the night under the stars of the Milky Way.

I set up a camp in a small cave on the limestone cliff overlooking the river. Gather a little firewood and go to catch supper.

I turn over several rocks and fallen logs, looking for grubs and worms. Finding none, I cut a sapling twice my height for a pole and go out onto a rock ledge that stands proud of the cliffs well over the river. I quietly creep out and look over the edge to see sunfish and crappie swimming in the deep pool of clear water far below. I gaze down and see fish and frogs and such, just as I have seen before from the bank, but now it is like watching a whole new world so far below and now see what I could not see before.

I see a large fish move imperceptibly slowly toward a frog that still has its polliwog tail. Flash of silver, and the frog is gone, just like that. The fish eats, and the frog dies. It is as if I am on the roof of the world watching life and death play out far, far below in another world. I ponder thoughts I do not comprehend as I push away from the precipice. I find a path down to the bank of the river and search for a pool my line will reach.

I still have no bait, but I will think of something.

Now, how will I tempt a couple of fish to be my supper? As I go down the path, I look again for something to use as bait. Finding nothing, I go ahead and prepare my pole anyway—I will think of something. I cut a notch in the tip, tie the string there, and tie the hook at the end of the string.

I still have no bait as I reach the high bank over the river where I can fish. It is too late in the fall for grasshoppers, and I cannot find any bugs at all. It has been a dry spell, and I suppose it has affected the fauna. I take out a stick of gum and fold up the foil and put it in my shirt pocket. I think, chew, and look around me, wondering what will fool a fish. Something to be an enticement to bite my hook. An idea comes to me. I take out the small piece of foil from the gum and wrap it around the hook, forming a ball shape for the head and a taper for the tail. I put a small twist into the tail and tie the lure to the hook just below the head with a piece of string. The tag ends of the string I unravel like wings.

Wow, it looks like a silver grub with wings. I would bite on that if I were a fish.

I watch intently as I drop the lure into the clear water, I see it flutter down to some fish and pass into deeper, darker water until the string is straight down. The fish ignore it until I pulled it back up. It spins and flashes, then several fish fight over the lure until one gets it in his mouth. *Wham,* I jerk the line and pull a hand-sized crappie out of the pool. It worked, and it works again when I bring in a larger fish. Surprised at how easily the fish are fooled, I pick up my pole and walk back to camp. Two fish are enough, so I clean them and broil them over the campfire using green limbs stuck in the dirt.

I lay out on the rock ledge after supper and gaze at the Milky Way while shooting stars streak across the sky. Now, as darkness covers me, I cannot see the river world below. The birth and life and death world, where one life feeding another fades into the darkness. The river world that fed me tonight knows nothing but the cycle of its existence. I doze off with a roof of sky above, with the Milky Way flowing like a river from primal to eternity. The wood, the river, and I are one. We sleep. We dream.

What a time to be a wild-child in the woods. I wonder if everyone feels this way, alone but not alone. The woods and river speak to me, the bounty of nature feeds me, and the peaceful blanket of primordial stars cover my fears as they have for every generation since Adam. I sleep and dream the ancient of dreams and trust my future to God.

Karl Smith is a local author, poet, pastor, college instructor of auto technology, and retired auto technician. He is the winner of many awards for his poetry, devotionals, and short stories. He is active in several area and state writing groups and a Counselor for the Poetry Society of Texas. Karl lives in Amarillo with his wife Judy. Together they serve as Support Humans for their two dogs, Teddy (Bear) and Smoky (Bear).

PARTING NOTES

If you enjoyed this collection of short stories and poetry, please consider purchasing one or more of our previous anthologies, leaving a kind review, and following your favorite authors on your favorite social media platform.

Previous Anthologies by
Texas High Plains Writers

With Words We Weave, 2019 Anthology
With Words We Weave: A Celebration of the Past, 2020 Centennial Anthology
With Words We Weave: Challenges, 2021 Anthology
With Words We Weave: Hope, 2022 Anthology
With Words We Weave: Survival, 2023 Anthology